I sprang to my feet, my hand grasping my pistol, my mind paralyzed by the dreadful shape which had sprung out upon us from the shadows of the fog.

A hound it was, an enormous coal-black hound, but not such a hound as mortal eyes have ever seen. Fire burst from its open mouth, its eyes glowed with a smoldering glare, its muzzle and neck were outlined in flickering flame. Never in the wildest dream of a madman could anything more savage, more terrible, more hellish be imagined than that dark form and savage face which broke upon us out of the wall of fog.

A Background Note about *The Hound of the Baskervilles*

The Hound of the Baskervilles takes place in England in the late 1800s. Although the story begins at Sherlock Holmes's comfortable apartment in London, most of the action takes place on the barren Devonshire moors of southwest England. This region of England had been settled long ago by prehistoric peoples who cleared the forest and established the first farming communities. The remains of their stone huts play a important part in the spooky setting of the story. At the time that A. Conan Doyle wrote the story, the Devonshire moors had experienced a long period of economic decline. The soil was too poor to support large-scale farming. In the 1870s the once important tin-mining industry went into a steep decline due to foreign competition. These factors only increased the gap between upper-class families such as the fictional Baskervilles and the impoverished common folk. Perhaps poverty and suspicion contributed to the legends and ghost stories which sprang up in the region. Whatever the cause, it's certain that Devonshire legends, such as one of a gigantic "hell-hound," provided author A. Conan Doyle with rich materials to create his famous mystery.

The HOUND of the BASKERVILLES

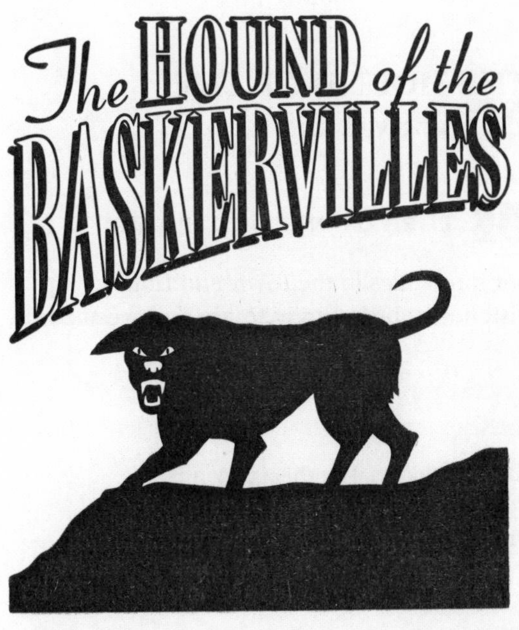

ARTHUR CONAN DOYLE

Edited, and with an Afterword,
by Ruth A. Rouff

 THE TOWNSEND LIBRARY

THE HOUND OF THE BASKERVILLES

TP THE TOWNSEND LIBRARY

For more titles in the Townsend Library,
visit our website: **www.townsendpress.com**

Printed in the United States of America

0 9 8 7 6 5 4 3 2

ISBN 13: 978-1-59194-064-7
ISBN 10: 1-59194-064-8

Library of Congress Control Number:
2005911002

Contents

CHAPTER 1

Mr. Sherlock Holmes

Mr. Sherlock Holmes was seated at the breakfast table. He usually got up very late in the mornings, except when he stayed up all night. I stood upon the fireplace rug and picked up the cane which our visitor had left behind him the night before. It was a fine, thick piece of wood, with a rounded head. Just under the head was a broad silver band nearly an inch across. "To James Mortimer, M.R.C.S., from his friends of the C.C.H.," was engraved upon it, with the date "1884." It was just the type of walking stick that old-fashioned family doctors used to carry—dignified, solid, and reassuring.

"Well, Watson, what do you make of it?"

Holmes was sitting with his back to me, and I had given him no sign of what I was doing.

"How did you know what I was doing? I believe you have eyes in the back of your head."

"I have, at least, a well-polished, silver-plated

coffee pot in front of me," said he. "But, tell me, Watson, what do you make of our visitor's cane? Since we have been so unfortunate as to miss him and have no idea why he came here, this accidental souvenir becomes important. Let me hear you reconstruct the man by examining it."

"I think," said I, following as far as I could the methods of my companion, "that Dr. Mortimer is a successful, elderly medical man, well-respected, since those who know him give him this mark of their appreciation."

"Good!" said Holmes. "Excellent!"

"I think also that he is probably a country doctor who does a great deal of his visiting on foot."

"Why so?"

"Because this cane, though originally a very fine one, has been knocked about so much that I can hardly imagine a town doctor carrying it. The thick iron cap at the bottom is worn down, so he has probably done a great amount of walking with it."

"Perfectly logical!" said Holmes.

"And then again, there is the 'friends of the C.C.H.' I would guess that to be the Something Hunt, the local hunt club. He has probably given some of the members medical assistance, and they have presented him a gift in return."

"Really, Watson, you outdo yourself," said Holmes, pushing back his chair and lighting a cigarette. "I am forced to say that in all the stories you have written about my small successes, you have constantly underrated your own abilities. It may be that you do not shed a great deal of light yourself, but you are a conductor of light. Some people who don't possess genius have a remarkable power of inspiring it. I confess, my dear fellow, that I owe a lot to you."

He had never said as much before, and I must admit that his words gave me keen pleasure. In the past, I had often been irritated by his indifference to my admiration and to the attempts which I had made to publicize his methods. I was proud, too, to think that I had mastered his system of making deductions well enough to apply it in a way which earned his approval. He now took the cane from my hands and examined it for a few minutes with his naked eyes. Then with an interested expression he laid down his cigarette, and carrying the cane to the window, he looked over it again with a magnifying glass.

"Interesting, though elementary," said he as he returned to his favorite corner of the sofa. "There are certainly one or two clues here which give us the basis for several deductions."

"Has anything escaped me?" I asked with some self-importance. "I trust that I have overlooked nothing important?"

"I am afraid, my dear Watson, that most of your conclusions were wrong. When I said that you inspired me I meant, to be blunt, that in noting your mistakes, I was sometimes guided toward the truth. Not that you are entirely wrong in this instance. The man is certainly a country doctor. And he walks a good deal."

"Then I was right."

"To that extent."

"But that was all."

"No, no, my dear Watson, not all—by no means all. I would suggest, for example, that a gift to a doctor is more likely to come from a hospital than from a hunt, and that when the initials 'C.C.' are placed before that hospital the words 'Charing Cross' very naturally come to mind."

"You may be right."

"Probably. And if we take this as a working hypothesis, we have a fresh basis to begin our construction of this unknown visitor."

"Well, then, supposing that 'C.C.H.' does stand for 'Charing Cross Hospital,' what further conclusions may we draw?"

"Do none suggest themselves? You know my methods. Apply them!"

"I can only think of the obvious conclusion that the man has practiced in town before going to the country."

"I think that we might infer a little more than this. Look at it in this way. When would it be most likely that such a presentation would be made? When would his friends unite to give him a token of their good will? Obviously at the moment when Dr. Mortimer withdrew from the service of the hospital in order to start in practice for himself. We know there has been a presentation. We believe there has been a change from a town hospital to a country practice. Is it, then, too much to say that the presentation was on the occasion of the change?"

"It certainly seems probable."

"Now, you will observe that he could not have been on the permanent staff of the hospital, since only a man well-established in a London practice could hold such a position. A person like that would not drift into the country. What was he, then? If he was in the hospital and yet not on the staff, he could only have been a house surgeon or a house physician—little more than a senior student. And he left five years ago—the date is on the cane. So your stern, middle-aged family practitioner vanishes into thin air, my dear Watson. The man who emerges in his place is a young fellow under thirty, good-natured, lacking in ambition, absent-minded, and the owner of a favorite dog, which I should describe roughly as being larger than a terrier and smaller than a mastiff."

I laughed in amazement as Sherlock Holmes leaned back in his sofa and blew little wavering rings of smoke up to the ceiling.

"As to the latter part, I have no means of checking you," said I, "but at least it is not difficult to find out a few facts about the man's age and professional career." From my small medical shelf I took down the Medical Directory and turned to the name. There were several Mortimers, but only one who could be our visitor. I read his record aloud.

"Mortimer, James, M.R.C.S., 1882, Grimpen, Dartmoor, Devon. House-surgeon, from 1882 to 1884, at Charing Cross Hospital. Winner of the Jackson prize for Comparative Pathology, with essay entitled 'Is Disease a Reversion?' Corresponding member of the Swedish Pathological Society. Author of 'Some Freaks of Genetics' (Lancet 1882). 'Do We Progress?' (Journal of Psychology, March, 1883). Medical Officer for the parishes of Grimpen, Thorsley, and High Barrow."

"No mention of that local hunt, Watson," said Holmes with a mischievous smile, "but a country doctor, as you very cleverly observed. I think that I am correct in my inferences. As to the adjectives, I said, if I remember right, good-natured, lacking in ambition, and absent-minded. It is my experience that it is only a good-natured man in this world who receives expressions of appreciation, only a man who lacks ambition who abandons a London career for the country, and only an absent-minded one who leaves his cane and not his visiting card after waiting an hour in your room."

"And the dog?"

"Has been in the habit of carrying this cane behind his master. Since it's a heavy cane, the dog has held it tightly by the middle, and the marks of his teeth are very plainly visible. The dog's jaw, as shown in the space between these marks, is too broad in my opinion for a terrier and not broad enough for a mastiff. It may have been—yes, by Jove, it is a curly-haired spaniel."

He had risen and paced the room as he spoke. Now he halted in the recess of the window. He sounded so certain of this fact that I glanced up in surprise.

"My dear fellow, how can you possibly be so sure of that?"

"For the very simple reason that I see the dog himself on our very doorstep, and there is the ring of its owner. Don't leave, I beg you, Watson. He is a professional brother of yours, and your presence may be helpful to me. Now is the fateful moment, Watson, when you hear a step upon the stair which is walking into your life, and you do not know whether it is for good or ill. What does Dr. James Mortimer, the man of science, ask of Sherlock Holmes, the specialist in crime? Come in!"

The appearance of our visitor was a surprise to me, since I had expected a typical country doctor. He was a very tall, thin man, with a long nose like a beak, which stuck out between two intelligent, gray eyes, set closely together and sparkling brightly from behind a pair of gold-rimmed glasses. He was dressed in a professional but rather sloppy manner, for his dress-coat was dirty and his trousers frayed. Though young, his long back was already bent, and he walked with his head thrust forward and a general air of peering kindliness. As he entered his eyes fell upon the cane in Holmes's hand, and he ran toward it with an exclamation of joy.

"I am so very glad," said he. "I was not sure whether I had left it here or in the Shipping Office. I would not lose that cane for the world."

"A gift, I see," said Holmes.

"Yes, sir."

"From Charing Cross Hospital?"

"From one or two friends there on the occasion of my marriage."

"Dear, dear, that's bad!" said Holmes, shaking his head.

Dr. Mortimer blinked through his glasses in mild astonishment.

"Why was it bad?"

"Only that you have disturbed our little deductions. Your marriage, you say?"

"Yes, sir. I married, and so left the hospital, and with it all hopes of a consulting practice. It was necessary to make a home of my own."

"Come, come, we are not so far wrong, after all," said Holmes. "And now, Dr. James

Mortimer—"

"Mister, sir, Mister—a humble M.R.C.S."

"And a man of precise mind, evidently."

"A dabbler in science, Mr. Holmes, a picker up of shells on the shores of the great unknown ocean. I believe that it is Mr. Sherlock Holmes whom I am addressing and not—"

"No, this is my friend Dr. Watson."

"Glad to meet you, sir. I have heard your name mentioned in connection with that of your friend. You interest me very much, Mr. Holmes. I had hardly expected your skull to be so long or your forehead to be so high. Would you have any objection to my running my finger along the middle of your skull? A cast of your skull, sir, until the original is available, would be a welcome addition to any natural science museum. It is not my intention to flatter you, but I confess that I desire your skull."

Sherlock Holmes waved our strange visitor into a chair. "You are enthusiastic about your specialty, I realize, sir, as I am in mine," said he. "I observe from your forefinger that you make your own cigarettes. Feel free to light one."

The man drew out paper and tobacco and twirled the one up in the other with surprising skill. He had long, quivering fingers, as energetic and restless as the antennae of an insect.

Holmes was silent, but his little darting glances showed me the interest which he took in our curious companion.

"I can guess, sir," he finally said, "that it was not merely for the purpose of examining my skull that you have done me the honor to call here last night and again today?"

"No, sir, no; though I am happy to have had the opportunity of doing that as well. I came to you, Mr. Holmes, because I recognized that I am myself an unpractical man and because I am suddenly faced with a most serious and extraordinary problem. Recognizing, as I do, that you are the second highest expert in Europe—"

"Indeed, sir! May I ask who has the honor to be the first?" asked Holmes with some sharpness.

"To the man of purely scientific mind, the work of Monsieur Bertillon must always appeal strongly."

"Then shouldn't you consult him?"

"I said, sir, to the purely scientific mind. But as a practical man of the world it is well known that you stand alone. I trust, sir, that I have not accidentally—"

"Just a little," said Holmes. "I think, Dr. Mortimer, it would be wise if you would simply tell me the exact nature of the problem you want me to help you with."

CHAPTER 2

The Curse of the Baskervilles

"I have in my pocket a manuscript," said Dr. James Mortimer.

"I observed it as you entered the room," said Holmes.

"It is an old manuscript."

"Early eighteenth century, unless it is a forgery."

"How can you say that, sir?"

"You have revealed an inch or two of it to my sight all the time that you have been talking. It would be a poor expert who could not give the date of a document within a decade or so. You may possibly have read my little article about the subject. I put that at 1730."

"The exact date is 1742." Dr. Mortimer removed it from his breast-pocket. "This family paper was given to me by Sir Charles Baskerville, whose sudden and tragic death some three months ago created so much excitement in

Devonshire. I may say that I was his personal friend as well as his medical attendant. He was a strong-minded man, sir, shrewd, practical, and as unimaginative as I am myself. Yet he took this document very seriously, and his mind was prepared for exactly what happened to him."

Holmes stretched out his hand for the manuscript and flattened it upon his knee.

"You will notice, Watson, that both the long version of the letter *s* and the short version are used. It is one of several characteristics which enabled me to decide on the date." I looked over his shoulder at the yellow paper and the faded writing. At the head was written: "Baskerville Hall," and below in large, scrawling figures: "1742."

"It appears to be a statement of some sort."

"Yes, it is a statement of a certain legend which runs in the Baskerville family."

"But I understand that it is something more modern and practical that you wish to ask me about?"

"Most modern. A most practical, urgent matter, which must be decided within twenty-four hours. But the manuscript is short and is very closely connected with the matter. With your permission I will read it to you."

Holmes leaned back in his chair, placed his fingertips together, and closed his eyes with an air of surrender. Dr. Mortimer turned the manuscript to the light and read in a high, crackling voice the following strange, old-world narrative:

"Of the origin of the Hound of the Baskervilles there have been many statements. Yet since I am a direct descendant of Hugo Baskerville, and since I heard the story from my father, who also heard it from his, I have written it down with the belief that it happened just as is here described. And I would have you believe, my sons, that the same Justice which punishes sin may also most graciously forgive it, and that no curse is so heavy but that by prayer and sincere apologies, it may be removed. Learn then from this story not to fear the fruits of the past, but rather to be careful in the future, so that those terrible passions which caused our family to suffer so horribly may not again lead to our downfall.

"Know then that in the time of the Great Rebellion (when we English overthrew King Charles I), this House of Baskerville was held by Hugo of that name. Nor can it be denied that he was a most wild, lustful, and godless man. This, in truth, his neighbors might have pardoned, seeing that there have never been many saints in those parts, but there was in him a certain recklessness and cruelty which gave him a bad reputation throughout the West. It happened that this Hugo came to love (if, indeed, so dark a passion may be known under so bright a name) the daughter of a gentleman farmer who held lands near the Baskerville estate. But the young maiden, being modest and of good reputation, would always avoid him, for she feared his evil name. So it happened that one day in late September, this Hugo, with five or six of his idle and wicked companions, stole down upon the farm and carried off the maiden, since he knew that her father and brothers were away at that time. When they had brought her to the Hall the maiden was placed in an upstairs room, while Hugo and his friends sat down to eat and get drunk, as was their nightly custom. Now, the poor lass who was held prisoner upstairs was nearly driven crazy by the singing and shouting and terrible curses which came up to her from below, for they say that Hugo Baskerville used to swear most terribly when he was drunk. At last, in the stress of her fear, she did something which might have frightened the bravest or most active man. With the aid of the ivy which covered (and still covers) the south wall, she climbed down to the ground, and began to walk homeward across the moor. There was about three miles between the Hall and her father's farm.

"It happened that a short while later, Hugo left his guests to carry food and drink—with other worse things, maybe—to his captive, and so found the cage empty and the bird escaped. Then, as it would seem, he became like one who is possessed by a devil. Rushing down the stairs into the dining hall, he jumped upon the great table, wine glasses and serving trays flying around him, and he cried aloud in front of everybody present that he would offer his body and soul to the Powers of Evil if he might only overtake the wench. And while the merrymakers stood amazed at the man's rage, one more wicked or, possibly, more drunk than the rest, cried out that they ought to set the hounds upon her. At this, Hugo ran from the house, shouting to his grooms that they should saddle his mare and release the pack. Giving the hounds a kerchief of the maid's, he swung them onto the trail, and so off they went, in full cry in the moonlight over the moor.

"Now, for some time the merrymakers stood open-mouthed, unable to understand all that had been done in such a hurry. But soon their confused wits awoke to the nature of the deed which was likely to be done upon the moorlands. Everything was now in an uproar, some calling for their pistols, some for their horses, and some for another flask of wine. But after a while, some sense came back to their crazed minds, and the whole of them, thirteen in number, took their horses and started off in pursuit. The moon shone clear above them, and they rode together swiftly, taking that course which the maid must have taken if she were to reach her own home.

"They had gone a mile or two when they passed one of the night shepherds upon the moorlands, and they shouted to him to ask if he had seen the hunt. And the man, as the story goes, was so crazed with fear that he could scarcely speak, but at last he said that he had indeed seen the unhappy maiden, with the hounds upon her track. 'But I have seen more than that,' said he, 'for Hugo Baskerville passed me upon his black mare, and there ran silently behind him such a hound of hell as God forbid should ever be at my heels.' So the drunken squires cursed the shepherd and rode onward. But soon their skins turned cold, for the sound of galloping came across the moor, and the black mare, dabbled with white sweat, went past with trailing bridle and empty saddle. Then the merry-makers rode close together, for they were very afraid. Still they followed over the moor, though each, had he been alone, would have been right glad to have turned his horse's head. Riding slowly in this fashion they came at last upon the hounds. These, though known for their bravery and their breeding, were whimpering in a cluster at the head of a deep dip in the moor. Some were slinking away and some, with raised fur and staring eyes, were gazing down the narrow valley in front of them.

"The company had come to a halt, more sober men, as you may guess, than when they started. Most of them would go no further, but three of them, the boldest, or it may be the most drunken, rode forward down into the valley. Now, it opened into a broad space in which stood two of those great stones, which can still be seen there, which were set by certain forgotten peoples in the days of old. The moon was shining bright upon the clearing, and there in the center lay the unhappy maid where she had fallen, dead of fear and exhaustion. But it was not the sight of her body, nor was it that of the body of Hugo Baskerville lying near her, which raised the hair upon the heads of these three daredevils. It was that, standing over Hugo, and tearing at his throat, there stood an evil thing, a great, black beast, shaped like a hound, yet larger than any hound that ever mortal eye has rested upon. And even as they looked, the thing tore the throat out of Hugo Baskerville. Then, as it turned its blazing eyes and dripping jaws upon them, the three shrieked with fear and rode for dear life, still screaming, across the moor. One, it is said, died that very night of what he had seen, and the other two were broken men for the rest of their days.

"Such is the tale, my sons, of the coming of the hound which is said to have tormented the family so terribly ever since. If I have set it down it is because that which is clearly known holds less terror than that which is but hinted at and guessed. Nor can it be denied that many of the family have been unlucky in their deaths, which have been sudden, bloody, and mysterious. Yet may we shelter ourselves in the infinite goodness of Providence, which would not forever punish the innocent. To that Providence, my sons, I hereby commend you, and I warn you not to cross the moor late at night when the forces of evil are most powerful.

"[This from Hugo Baskerville to his sons Rodger and John, with instructions that they say nothing thereof to their sister Elizabeth.]"

When Dr. Mortimer had finished reading this highly unusual narrative he pushed his spectacles up on his forehead and stared across at Mr. Sherlock Holmes. The latter yawned and tossed the end of his cigarette into the fire.

"Well?" said he.

"Do you not find it interesting?"

"To a collector of fairy tales."

Dr. Mortimer drew a folded newspaper out of his pocket.

"Now, Mr. Holmes, I will read you something a little more recent. This is the Devon County Chronicle of May 14th of this year. It is a short account of the facts brought forth at the death of Sir Charles Baskerville which occurred a few days before that date."

My friend leaned a little forward and his expression became intent. Our visitor readjusted his glasses and began:

"The recent sudden death of Sir Charles Baskerville has cast a gloom over the county. Though Sir Charles had lived at Baskerville Hall for a relatively short time, his friendliness and extreme generosity had won the affection and respect of all who came to know him. In these days of newly rich people, it is refreshing to find a case where the descendant of an old county family which has fallen upon evil days is able to make his own fortune and to bring it back with him to restore the fallen greatness of his ancestors. Sir Charles, as is well known, made large sums of money in South African investments. Wiser than those who keep investing until fortune turns against them, he cashed in his gains and returned to England with them. It has only been two years since he began living at Baskerville Hall, and it is common talk how large were those plans of reconstruction and improvement which have been interrupted by his death. Since he was childless, it was his openly expressed desire that the whole countryside should, within his own lifetime, profit by his good fortune. Many will have personal reasons for mourning his untimely end. His generous donations to local and county charities have often been written about in these columns.

"The circumstances connected with the death of Sir Charles weren't entirely cleared up by the investigation, but at least enough has been done to discredit the local superstitions. There is no reason whatever to suspect foul play, or to imagine that death could be from any but natural causes. Sir Charles was a widower, and a man who, it was said, had some odd personal habits. In spite of his considerable wealth, he had simple tastes. His indoor servants at Baskerville Hall were a married couple named Barrymore. The husband acted as butler and the wife as housekeeper. Their evidence, supported by that of several friends, tends to show that Sir Charles had health problems for quite a while, and points especially to heart disease. The symptoms of this illness were changes in complexion, breathlessness, and severe attacks of nervous depression. Dr. James Mortimer, the friend and medical attendant of the deceased, has given evidence which supports this conclusion.

"The facts of the case are simple. Sir Charles Baskerville had the habit every night before going to bed of walking down the famous yew alley of Baskerville Hall. The evidence of the Barrymores shows that this had been his habit. On the fourth of May Sir Charles had declared his intention of starting next day for London, and had ordered Barrymore to prepare his luggage. That night he went out as usual for his nightly walk, during which he was in the habit of smoking a cigar. He never returned. At twelve o'clock Barrymore, finding the hall door still open, became alarmed, and, lighting a lantern, went in search of his master. The day had been wet, and Sir Charles's footprints were easily traced down the alley. Halfway down this walk there is a gate which leads out on to the moor. There were signs that Sir Charles had stood there for a short while. He then continued down the alley, and it was at the far end of it that his body was discovered. One fact which has not been explained is the statement of Barrymore that his master's footprints changed in appearance from the time that he passed the moor gate, and that he appeared from there onward to have been walking upon his toes. A man named Murphy, a gypsy horse-dealer, was on the moor a short distance away at the time, but he appears by his own confession to have been quite drunk. He declares that he heard cries but is unable to state from what direction they came. No signs of violence were discovered upon Sir Charles's body, and the doctor's evidence pointed to an almost incredible facial distortion—so great that Dr. Mortimer refused at first to believe that it was indeed his friend and patient who lay before him. It was, however, explained that this is a symptom which is fairly common in cases of death from heart disease. This explanation was confirmed by the post-mortem examination, which showed long-standing heart disease, and the coroner's jury returned a verdict which agreed with the medical evidence.

It is good that this is so, for it is obviously of the greatest importance that Sir Charles's heir should settle down at the Hall and continue the good work which has been so sadly interrupted. If the coroner hadn't put the cause of death as natural causes and thereby put an end to the rumors which have been whispered in connection with the affair, it might have been difficult to find a tenant for Baskerville Hall. It has been learned that the next of kin is Mr. Henry Baskerville, the son of Sir Charles Baskerville's younger brother. The young man was last known to be in America, and attempts are being made to locate him and inform him of his good fortune."

Dr. Mortimer refolded his paper and replaced it in his pocket.

"Those are the public facts, Mr. Holmes, in connection with the death of Sir Charles Baskerville."

"I must thank you," said Sherlock Holmes, "for calling my attention to a case which certainly seems challenging. I had read a few newspaper reports at the time, but I was very busy with that little case at the Vatican, and in my eagerness to assist the Pope I lost touch with several interesting English cases. This article, you say, contains all the public facts?"

"It does."

"Then let me have the private ones." He leaned back, put his fingertips together, and put on his most emotionless and judge-like expression.

"In doing so," said Dr. Mortimer, who had begun to show signs of some strong emotion, "I am telling you something which I have not told anyone. My reason for not mentioning it during the coroner's inquiry is that a man of science doesn't like to seem to publicly support a popular superstition. I also reasoned that Baskerville Hall, as the paper says, would certainly remain unoccupied if anything were done to increase its already rather grim reputation. For both these reasons I thought that I had better tell a bit less than I knew, since no practical good could result from it. However with you there is no reason why I should not be perfectly open.

"Very few people live on the moor, and those who live near each other are thrown very much together. For this reason I saw a good deal of Sir Charles Baskerville. With the exception of Mr. Frankland, of Lafter Hall, and Mr. Stapleton, the naturalist, there are no other educated men within miles. Sir Charles was a shy man, but his illness brought us together, and our interest in science kept us together. He had brought back much scientific information from South Africa, and we used to spend many pleasant evenings together discussing the comparative anatomy of the Bushman and the Hottentot tribesmen."

"Within the last few months it became increasingly plain to me that Sir Charles was close to suffering a nervous breakdown. He had taken this legend which I have read you very much to heart—so much so that, although he would walk in his own grounds, nothing would convince him to go out upon the moor at night. Incredible as it may appear to you, Mr. Holmes, he was honestly convinced that a dreadful fate overhung his family. Certainly the records he had of his ancestors were not encouraging. The idea of some awful presence constantly haunted him, and on more than one occasion he has asked me whether, when I was performing a medical house-call at night, I had ever seen any strange creature or heard the baying of a hound. He asked me the second question several times, and always with a voice which vibrated with excitement.

"I can clearly remember driving up to his house in the evening some three weeks before the fatal event. He happened to be at his hall door. I had descended from my coach and was standing in front of him, when I saw his eyes fix themselves over my shoulder and stare past me with an expression of the most dreadful horror. I turned around just in time to catch a glimpse of something which I took to be a large black calf passing at the head of the drive. So excited and alarmed was he that I was forced to go down to the spot where the animal had been and look around for it. It was gone, however, and the incident appeared to affect him terribly. I stayed with him all evening, and it was at that time, to explain the emotion which he had shown, that he game me that narrative which I read to you when I first arrived. I mention this small incident because it seems important in view of the tragedy which followed. However, I was convinced at the time that the matter was totally unimportant and that his excitement was unreasonable.

"I was the one who advised Sir Charles to go to London. His heart was, I knew, affected, and the constant anxiety in which he lived, however unreal the cause of it might be, was evidently having a serious effect upon his health. I thought that a few months among the amusements of town would make him a new man. Mr. Stapleton, a friend to both of us, who was much concerned about the state of his health, had the same opinion. At the last instant came this terrible catastrophe.

"On the night of Sir Charles's death, Barrymore the butler who made the discovery, sent Perkins the groom on horseback to me. Since I was sitting up late, I was able to reach Baskerville Hall within an hour of the event. I checked and confirmed all the facts which were mentioned at the inquest. I followed the footsteps down the yew alley, I saw the spot at the moor gate where he seemed to have waited, I noticed the change in the shape of the prints after that point, I noted that there were no other footsteps except those of Barrymore on the soft gravel, and finally I carefully examined the body, which had not been touched until my arrival. Sir Charles lay on his face, his arms out, and his fingers dug into the ground. His features were so twisted with horror that I hardly recognized him. There was certainly no physical injury of any kind. But one false statement was made by Barrymore at the inquest. He said that there were no traces upon the ground around the body. He did not notice any. But I did—a short distance away, but fresh and clear."

"Footprints?"

"Footprints."

"A man's or a woman's?"

Dr. Mortimer looked strangely at us for an instant, and his voice sank almost to a whisper as he answered:

"Mr. Holmes, they were the footprints of a gigantic hound!"

CHAPTER 3

The Problem

I confess at these words a shudder passed through me. There was a shiver in the doctor's voice which showed that he was himself deeply moved by that which he told us. Holmes leaned forward in his excitement and his eyes had the hard, dry glitter which shot from them when he was deeply interested.

"You saw this?"

"As clearly as I see you."

"And you said nothing?"

"What was the use?"

"How was it that no one else saw it?"

"The marks were some twenty yards from the body and no one gave them a thought. I don't suppose I would have done so had I not known this legend."

"There are many sheepdogs on the moor?"

"No doubt, but this was no sheepdog."

"You say it was large?"

"Enormous."

"But it had not approached the body?"

"No."

"What sort of night was it?"

"Damp and cold."

"But not actually raining?"

"No."

"What is the alley like?"

"There are two lines of old yew hedge, twelve feet high and impassable. The walk in the center is about eight feet across."

"Is there anything between the hedges and the walk?"

"Yes, there is a strip of grass about six feet broad on either side."

"I understand that there is a gate in the yew hedge?"

"Yes, the wicket gate which leads on to the moor."

"Is there any other opening?"

"None."

"So that to reach the yew alley one either has to come down it from the house or else to enter it by the moor gate?"

"There is an exit through a summer house at the far end."

"Had Sir Charles reached this?"

"No; he lay about fifty yards from it."

"Now, tell me, Dr. Mortimer—and this is important—the marks which you saw were on the path and not on the grass?"

"No marks could show on the grass."

"Were they on the same side of the path as the moor gate?"

"Yes; they were on the edge of the path on the same side as the moor gate."

"You interest me very much. Another point. Was the wicket gate closed?"

"Closed and padlocked."

"How high was it?"

"About four feet high."

"Then anyone could have got over it?"

"Yes."

"And what marks did you see by the wicket gate?"

"None in particular."

"Good heaven! Did no one examine?"

"Yes, I examined it, myself."

"And found nothing?"

"It was all very confused. Sir Charles had evidently stood there for five or ten minutes."

"How do you know that?"

"Because the ash had twice dropped from his cigar."

"Excellent! This is a man, Watson, who thinks like us. But the marks?"

"He had left his own marks all over that small patch of gravel. I could see no others."

Sherlock Holmes struck his hand against his knee with an impatient gesture.

"If I had only been there!" he cried. "It is

evidently a case of tremendous interest, and one which presented great opportunities to the scientific expert. That gravel page upon which I might have read so much has been already smudged by the rain and defaced by the shoes of curious local folk. Oh, Dr. Mortimer, Dr. Mortimer, to think that you didn't call me in! You have much to answer for, indeed."

"I could not call you in, Mr. Holmes, without revealing these facts to the world, and I have already given my reasons for not wishing to do so. Besides, besides—"

"Why do you hesitate?"

"There is an area in which the most brilliant and most experienced of detectives is helpless."

"You mean that the thing is supernatural?"

"I did not positively say so."

"No, but you evidently think it."

"Since the tragedy, Mr. Holmes, I've heard of several incidents which don't agree with the settled order of Nature."

"For example?"

"I find that before the terrible event occurred, several people had seen a creature upon the moor which sounds like this Baskerville demon, and which could not possibly be any animal known to science. They all agreed that it was a huge creature, glowing, hideous, and ghost-like. I have cross-examined these men, one of them a hard-headed countryman, one a horse doctor, and one a moorland farmer, who all tell the same story of this dreadful phantom, exactly matching the hell-hound of the legend. I assure you that there is a reign of terror in the district, and that it is a brave man who will cross the moor at night."

"And you, a trained man of science, believe it to be supernatural?"

"I do not know what to believe."

Holmes shrugged his shoulders.

"Until now I have confined my investigations to this world," said he. "In a modest way I have combated evil, but to take on the Father of Evil himself would, perhaps, be too challenging a task. Yet you must admit that the footmark is real."

"The original hound was real enough to rip a man's throat out, and yet he was devilish as well."

"I see that you have gone over to the side of the supernaturalists. But now, Dr. Mortimer, tell me this. If you hold these views why have you come to ask my help at all? You tell me in the same breath that it is useless to investigate Sir Charles's death, and that you wish me to do it."

"I did not say that I wished you to do it."

"Then, how can I help you?"

"By advising me as to what I should do with Sir Henry Baskerville, who arrives at Waterloo Station"—Dr. Mortimer looked at his watch—"in exactly one hour and a quarter."

"He is the heir?"

"Yes. On the death of Sir Charles we searched for this young gentleman and found that he had been farming in Canada. From the accounts which have reached us, he is an excellent fellow in every way. I speak now not as a medical man but as a trustee and executor of Sir Charles's will."

"There is no other relative who could claim the estate, I presume?"

"None. The only other kinsman whom we have been able to trace was Rodger Baskerville, the youngest of three brothers of whom poor Sir Charles was the oldest. The second brother, who died young, is the father of this lad Henry. The third, Rodger, was the black sheep of the family. He behaved like the old and fearsome Baskervilles and looked very much like the family picture of old Hugo. He got into trouble with the law in England, fled to Central America, and died there in 1876 of yellow fever. Henry is the last of the Baskervilles. In one hour and five minutes I will meet him at Waterloo Station. I received a telegram that he arrived at Southampton this morning. Now, Mr. Holmes, what would you advise me to do with him?"

"Why shouldn't he go to the home of his fathers?"

"It seems natural, does it not? And yet, consider that every Baskerville who goes there meets with an evil fate. I feel sure that if Sir Charles could have spoken with me before his death, he would have warned me against bringing Henry Baskerville to that deadly place. And yet it cannot be denied that the prosperity of the whole poor, bleak countryside depends upon his presence. All the good work which has been done by Sir Charles will crash to the ground if there is no one to occupy the Hall. I am prejudiced in this regard, and that is why I bring the case before you and ask for your advice."

Holmes considered for a little time.

"Put into plain words, the matter is this," he said. "In your opinion there is a devilish power which makes Dartmoor an unsafe home for a Baskerville—that is your opinion?"

"At least I might go the length of saying that there is some evidence that this may be so."

"Exactly. But surely, if your supernatural theory is correct, it could work the young man evil in London as easily as in Devonshire. A devil with only local powers like a parish priest would be too hard to believe."

"You treat the matter more lightly, Mr. Holmes, than you would probably do if you had personal contact with these things. Your advice, then, as I understand it, is that the young man will be as safe in Devonshire as in London. He comes in fifty minutes. What do you recommend?"

"I recommend, sir, that you take a cab, call off your spaniel who is scratching at my front door, and go to Waterloo to meet Sir Henry

Baskerville."

"And then?"

"And then you will say nothing to him at all until I have made up my mind about the matter."

"How long will it take you to make up your mind?"

"Twenty-four hours. At ten o'clock tomorrow, Dr. Mortimer, I will be much obliged to you if you will call upon me here. Also, it will be helpful to me in my plans for the future if you will bring Sir Henry Baskerville with you."

"I will do so, Mr. Holmes." He scribbled the appointment on his shirt cuff and hurried off in his strange, peering, absentminded fashion. Holmes stopped him at the head of the stair.

"Only one more question, Dr. Mortimer. You say that before Sir Charles Baskerville's death, several people saw this phantom out on the moor?"

"Three people did."

"Did any of them see it afterward?"

"I haven't heard of any."

"Thank you. Good morning."

Holmes returned to his seat with that quiet look of inward satisfaction which meant that he had an agreeable task ahead of him.

"Going out, Watson?"

"Unless I can help you."

"No, my dear fellow, it is at the hour of action that I turn to you for aid. But this is wonderful, really unequalled from some points of view. When you pass Bradley's, would you ask him to send up a pound of the strongest shredded tobacco? Thank you. It would be good, also, if you didn't return before evening. Then I would be very glad to share my thoughts with you regarding this most interesting problem which has been given to us this morning."

I knew that it was very necessary for my friend to be alone in those hours. When he was alone, he could weigh each piece of evidence, construct alternative theories, balance one against the other, and make up his mind as to which points were essential and which unimportant. I therefore spent the day at my club and did not return to Baker Street until evening. It was nearly nine o'clock when I found myself in the sitting room once more.

My first impression as I opened the door was that a fire had broken out. The room was so filled with smoke that the lamplight appeared blurry. As I entered, however, my fears were set at rest, for it was the bitter fumes of strong, coarse tobacco which took me by the throat and set me coughing. Through the haze, I could barely see Holmes in his dressing gown coiled up in an armchair with his black clay pipe between his lips. Several rolls of paper lay around him.

"Caught cold, Watson?" said he.

"No, it's this poisonous atmosphere."

"I suppose it is pretty thick, now that you mention it."

"Thick! It is unbearable."

"Open the window, then! You have been at your club all day, I see."

"My dear Holmes!"

"Am I right?"

"Certainly, but how?"

He laughed at my bewildered expression.

"There is a delightful freshness about you, Watson, which makes it a pleasure to use my abilities at your expense. A gentleman goes out on a damp and gray day. He returns in the evening with the shine still on his hat and his boots. He has been in the same place, therefore, all day. He is not a man with close friends. Where, then, could he have been? Isn't it clear?"

"Well, it is rather obvious."

"The world is full of obvious things which nobody ever observes. Where do you think that I have been?"

"In the same place, also."

"On the contrary, I have been to Devonshire."

"In spirit?"

"Exactly. My body has remained in this armchair and has, I reluctantly admit, consumed in my absence two large pots of coffee and an incredible amount of tobacco. After you left I sent down to Stamford's for a detailed map of this part of the moor, and my spirit has hovered over it all day. I flatter myself that I could find my way about."

"A large-scale map, I imagine?"

"Very large." He unrolled one section and held it over his knee. "Here you have the particular district which concerns us. That is Baskerville Hall in the middle."

"With a forest around it?"

"Exactly. I believe the yew alley, though not marked under that name, must stretch along this line, with the moor, as you see, upon the right of it. This small clump of buildings here is the village of Grimpen, where our friend Dr. Mortimer has his headquarters. Within a radius of five miles there are, as you see, only a very few scattered houses. Here is Lafter Hall, which was mentioned in the story. There is a house indicated here which may be the residence of the naturalist—Stapleton, if I remember right, was his name. Here are two moorland farmhouses, High Tor and Foulmire. Then fourteen miles away the great convict prison of Princetown. Between and around these scattered points extends the bleak, lifeless moor. This, then, is the stage upon which tragedy has been played, and upon which we may help to play it again."

"It must be a wild place."

"Yes, the setting is a worthy one. If the devil did desire to have a hand in the affairs of men—"

"Then you are yourself leaning toward the

supernatural explanation."

"The devil's helpers may be of flesh and blood, may they not? There are two questions waiting for us at the beginning. One question is whether any crime has been committed at all. The second question is what is the crime and how was it committed? Of course, if Dr. Mortimer's guess is correct, and we are dealing with forces outside the ordinary laws of Nature, that ends our investigation. But we should rule out all other theories before falling back upon this one. I think we'll shut that window again, if you don't mind. It is a strange thing, but I find that thick air encourages deep thought. I have not pushed it to the length of getting into a box to think, but that is the logical outcome of my beliefs."

"Have you turned the case over in your mind?"

"Yes, I have thought a good deal of it in the course of the day."

"What do you make of it?"

"It is very puzzling."

"It has certainly a character of its own. There are points which stand out. That change in the footprints, for example. What do you make of that?"

"Mortimer said that the man had walked on tiptoe down that portion of the alley."

"He only repeated what some fool had said at the inquest. Why should a man walk on tiptoe down the alley?"

"What then?"

"He was running, Watson—running desperately, running for his life, running until he burst his heart and fell dead upon his face."

"Running from what?"

"There lies our problem. There are signs that the man was crazed with fear before ever he began to run."

"How can you say that?"

"I believe that the cause of his fears came to him across the moor. If that were so, and it seems most probable only a man who had lost his wits would have run from the house instead of toward it. If the gypsy's evidence may be taken as true, he ran with cries for help in the direction where help was least likely to be. Then, again, who was he waiting for that night, and why was he waiting for him in the yew alley rather than in his own house?"

"You think that he was waiting for someone?"

"The man was elderly and in poor health. We can understand his taking an evening stroll, but the ground was damp and the night stormy. Is it natural that he should stand for five or ten minutes, as Dr. Mortimer concluded from the cigar ash?"

"But he went out every evening."

"I think it is unlikely that he waited at the

moor gate every evening. On the contrary, the evidence is that he avoided the moor. That night he waited there. It was the night before he left for London. The thing takes shape, Watson. It becomes meaningful. Might I ask you to hand me my violin, and we will postpone all further thought upon this business until we have had the advantage of meeting Dr. Mortimer and Sir Henry Baskerville in the morning."

CHAPTER 4

Sir Henry Baskerville

Our breakfast table was cleared early, and Holmes waited in his dressing gown for the promised discussion. Our clients were on time for their appointment. The clock had just struck ten when Dr. Mortimer was shown up, followed by the young baronet. The latter was a small, alert, dark-eyed man about thirty years old, very sturdily built, with thick black eyebrows and a strong, defiant-looking face. He wore a ruddy-tinted tweed suit and had the weather-beaten appearance of one who has spent most of his time in the open air. Yet there was something in his steady eye and the quiet confidence of his bearing which suggested that he was a gentleman.

"This is Sir Henry Baskerville," said Dr. Mortimer.

"Why, yes," said he, "and the strange thing is, Mr. Sherlock Holmes, that if my friend here had not suggested coming around to you this morning, I would have come on my own. I understand that you think about little puzzles, and I've had one this morning which needs more thinking about than I am able to give it."

"Please take a seat, Sir Henry. Do I understand you to say that you have had some remarkable experience since you arrived in London?"

"Nothing of much importance, Mr. Holmes. Only a joke, probably. It was this letter, if you can call it a letter, which reached me this morning."

He laid an envelope upon the table, and we all bent over it. It was of average quality, grayish in color. The address, "Sir Henry Baskerville, Northumberland Hotel," was printed in rough letters; the postmark "Charing Cross," and the mailing date was the past evening.

"Who knew that you were going to the Northumberland Hotel?" asked Holmes, glancing intently across at our visitor.

"No one could have known. We only decided after I met Dr. Mortimer."

"But Dr. Mortimer was no doubt already staying there?"

"No, I had been staying with a friend," said the doctor. "There was no possible notice that we intended to go to this hotel."

"Hum! Someone seems to be very deeply interested in your movements." Out of the envelope he took a half-sheet of writing paper, which had been folded into quarters. This he opened and spread flat upon the table. Across the middle of it a single sentence had been formed by pasting printed words upon it. It ran:

> If you value your life or your reason keep away from the moor.

The word "moor" only was printed in ink.

"Now," said Sir Henry Baskerville, "perhaps you will tell me, Mr. Holmes, what in thunder is the meaning of that, and who it is that takes so much interest in my affairs?"

"What do you make of it, Dr. Mortimer? You must admit that there is nothing supernatural about this, at any rate?"

"No, sir, but it might very well come from someone who was convinced that the business is supernatural."

"What business?" asked Sir Henry sharply. "It seems to me that all you gentlemen know a great deal more than I do about my own business."

"You shall share our knowledge before you leave this room, Sir Henry. I promise you that," said Sherlock Holmes. "But at this point, let's focus on this very interesting document, which must have been put together and mailed yesterday evening. Do you have yesterday's *Times*, Watson?"

"It is here in the corner."

"Might I trouble you for it—the inside page, please, with the leading articles?" He glanced swiftly over it, running his eyes up and down the columns.

"Here's an interesting article on free trade. Permit me to read you a part of it:

"'You may be bullied into imagining that your own special trade or your own industry will be helped by a protective tariff, but it stands to reason that such laws must in the long run keep away wealth from the country, lessen the value of our imports, and lower the general conditions of life in this island.'"

"What do you think of that, Watson?" cried Holmes happily, rubbing his hands together with satisfaction. "Don't you think that is an admirable opinion?"

Dr. Mortimer looked at Holmes with an air of professional interest, and Sir Henry Baskerville turned a pair of puzzled dark eyes upon me.

"I don't know much about the tariff and things of that kind," said he, "but it seems to me we've got a bit off the trail so far as that note is concerned."

"On the contrary, I think we are particularly hot upon the trail, Sir Henry. Watson here knows more about my methods than you do, but I fear that even he has not quite grasped the importance of this sentence."

"No, I confess that I see no connection."

"And yet, my dear Watson, there is so very close a connection that the one is extracted out of the other. 'You,' 'your,' 'your,' 'life,' 'reason,' 'value,' 'keep away,' 'from the.' Don't you see now where these words come from?"

"By thunder, you're right! Well, if that isn't smart!" cried Sir Henry.

"If any possible doubt remained it is settled by the fact that 'keep away' and 'from the' are cut out in one piece."

"Well, now—so it is!"

"Really, Mr. Holmes, this exceeds anything which I could have imagined," said Dr. Mortimer, gazing at my friend in amazement. "I could understand anyone saying that the words were from a newspaper; but that you should name which, and add that it came from the leading article, is really one of the most remarkable things which I have ever known. How did you do it?"

"I believe, Doctor, that you could tell the skull of a Negro from that of an Eskimo?"

"Most certainly."

"But how?"

"Because that is my special hobby. The differences are obvious. The eyebrow ridge, the facial angle, the jaw line, the—"

"But this is my special hobby, and the differences are equally clear. There is as much difference to my eyes between the leaded typeface of a *Times* article and the sloppy print of an evening half-penny paper as there could be between your Negro and your Eskimo. The detection of typefaces is one of the most elementary branches of knowledge to the expert in crime, although I confess that once when I was very young I confused the *Leeds Mercury* with the *Western Morning News.* But a *Times* editorial is very distinctive, and these words could have been taken from nothing else. As it was done yesterday, it was highly likely that we would find the words in yesterday's issue."

"So far as I can follow you, then, Mr. Holmes," said Sir Henry Baskerville, "someone cut out this message with a scissors—"

"Nail scissors," said Holmes. "You can see that it was a very short-bladed scissors, since the cutter had to take two snips over 'keep away.'"

"That is so. Someone, then, cut out the message with a pair of short-bladed scissors, pasted it with paste—"

"Glue," said Holmes.

"With glue on to the paper. But I want to know why the word 'moor' should have been written?"

"Because he could not find it in print. The other words were all simple and might be found in any issue, but 'moor' would be less common."

"Why, of course, that would explain it. Have you noticed anything else in this message, Mr. Holmes?"

"There are one or two clues, even though whoever did it tried hard to remove all clues. The address, you notice, is printed in rough letters.

But the *Times* is a paper which is usually read by highly educated people. We may believe, therefore, that the letter was composed by an educated man who wished to pretend to be an uneducated one. His effort to hide his own writing suggests that that writing might be known, or come to be known, by you. Again, you will notice that the words are not glued on in a straight line, but that some are much higher than others. 'Life,' for example is really out of its proper place. That may point to carelessness or it may suggest that the cutter was nervous and in a hurry. On the whole, I lean to the latter view, since the matter was certainly important, and it is unlikely that the composer of such a letter would be careless. If he were in a hurry, it opens up the interesting question why he should be in a hurry, since any letter mailed up to early morning would reach Sir Henry before he would leave his hotel. Did the person who created this message fear an interruption—and from whom?"

"We are coming now into an area of guesswork," said Dr. Mortimer.

"Say, rather, into an area where we balance probabilities and choose the most likely. It is the scientific use of the imagination, but we always have some solid facts on which to start our thinking. Now, you would call it a guess, no doubt, but I am almost certain that this address has been written in a hotel."

"How in the world can you say that?"

"If you examine it carefully you will see that both the pen and the ink have given the writer trouble. The pen has spluttered twice in a single word and has run dry three times in a short address. This demonstrates that there was very little ink in the bottle. Now, a private pen or ink bottle is rarely allowed to run dry, and the combination of the two must be quite rare. But you know what hotel ink and hotel pens are like. Yes, I have very little doubt in saying that if we could examine the wastebaskets of the hotels around Charing Cross until we found the remains of the cut-up *Times* editorial, we could quickly lay our hands upon the person who sent this unusual message. Hello! Hello! What's this?"

He was carefully examining the writing paper, upon which the words were pasted, holding it only an inch or two from his eyes.

"Well?"

"Nothing," said he, throwing it down. "It is a blank half-sheet of paper, without even a watermark upon it. I think we have learned as much as we can from this strange letter. And now, Sir Henry, has anything else of interest happened to you since you have been in London?"

"Why, no, Mr. Holmes. I think not."

"You have not noticed anyone follow or watch you?"

"I seem to have walked right into the pages

of a dime novel," said our visitor. "Why in thunder should anyone follow or watch me?"

"We are coming to that. You have nothing else to report to us before we go into this matter?"

"Well, it depends upon what you think worth reporting."

"I think anything out of the ordinary well worth reporting."

Sir Henry smiled.

"I don't know much about British life yet, for I have spent nearly all my time in the States and in Canada. But I hope that to lose one of your boots is not part of the ordinary routine over here."

"You have lost one of your boots?"

"My dear sir," cried Dr. Mortimer, "it is only misplaced. You will find it when you return to the hotel. What is the use of troubling Mr. Holmes with trivia of this kind?"

"Well, he asked me for anything outside the ordinary routine."

"Exactly," said Holmes, "however foolish the incident may seem. You have lost one of your boots, you say?"

"Well, misplaced it, anyhow. I put them both outside my door last night, and there was only one in the morning. I could get no answer out of the chap who cleans them. The worst of it is that I only bought the pair last night in the Strand shopping district, and I have never had them on."

"If you have never worn them, why did you put them out to be cleaned?"

"They were tan boots and had never been waterproofed. That was why I put them out."

"Then I understand that on your arrival in London yesterday you went out at once and bought a pair of boots?"

"I did a good deal of shopping. Dr. Mortimer here went around with me. You see, if I am to be a titled landowner down there I must dress the part, and it may be that I have gotten a little careless in my ways out West. Among other things I bought these brown boots—paid six dollars for them—and had one stolen before ever I had them on my feet."

"It seems a remarkably useless thing to steal," said Sherlock Holmes. "I confess that I share Dr. Mortimer's belief that it will not be long before the missing boot is found."

"And, now, gentlemen," said the baronet with decision, "it seems to me that I have spoken quite enough about the little that I know. It is time that you kept your promise and gave me a full account of what we are all getting at."

"Your request is a very reasonable one," Holmes answered. "Dr. Mortimer, I think you could not do better than to tell your story as you told it to us."

Thus encouraged, our scientific friend drew his papers from his pocket and presented the whole case as he had done the morning before. Sir Henry Baskerville listened with the deepest attention and with an occasional exclamation of surprise.

"Well, I seem to have come into an inheritance in more ways than one," he said when the long story was finished. "Of course, I've heard of the hound ever since I was in the nursery. It's the pet story of the family, though I never thought of taking it seriously before. But as to my uncle's death—well, it all seems to be boiling up in my head, and I can't get it clear yet. You don't seem quite to have made up your mind whether it's a case for a policeman or a minister."

"Exactly."

"And now there's this business of the letter to me at the hotel. I suppose that fits into its place."

"It seems to show that someone knows more than we do about what goes on upon the moor," said Dr. Mortimer.

"And also," said Holmes, "that someone looks kindly on you, since they warn you of danger."

"Or it may be that they wish, for their own purposes, to scare me away."

"Well, of course, that is possible also. I am very much indebted to you, Dr. Mortimer, for introducing me to a problem which presents several interesting alternatives. But the practical point which we now have to decide, Sir Henry, is whether you should or should not go to Baskerville Hall."

"Why shouldn't I go?"

"There seems to be danger."

"Do you mean danger from this family demon or do you mean danger from human beings?"

"Well, that is what we have to find out."

"Whichever it is, my answer is fixed. There is no devil in hell, Mr. Holmes, and there is no man upon earth who can prevent me from going to the home of my own people. You may take that to be my final answer." His dark brows knitted and his face flushed to a dusky red as he spoke. It was evident that the fiery temper of the Baskervilles still survived in this, their last representative.

"Meanwhile," said he, "I have hardly had time to think over all that you have told me. It's a big thing for a man to have to understand and to decide at one sitting. I would like to have a quiet hour by myself to make up my mind. Now, look here, Mr. Holmes, it's half-past eleven now and I am going back right away to my hotel. Suppose you and your friend, Dr. Watson, come around and lunch with us at two. I'll be able to tell you more clearly then how this thing strikes me."

"Is that convenient to you, Watson?"

"Perfectly."

"Then you may expect us. Shall I have a cab called?"

"I'd prefer to walk, for this business has excited me."

"I'll join you in a walk, with pleasure," said his companion.

"Then we meet again at two o'clock. Goodbye, and good morning!"

We heard the steps of our visitors descend the stair and the bang of the front door. In an instant Holmes had changed from the slow-moving dreamer to the man of action.

"Your hat and boots, Watson, quick! Not a moment to lose!" He rushed into his room in his dressing gown and was back again in a few seconds in an overcoat. We hurried together down the stairs and into the street. Dr. Mortimer and Baskerville were still visible about two hundred yards ahead of us in the direction of Oxford Street.

"Shall I run on and stop them?"

"Not for the world, my dear Watson. I am perfectly satisfied with your company if you will put up with mine. Our friends are wise, for it is certainly a very fine morning for a walk."

He quickened his pace until we had narrowed the distance which divided us by about half. Then, still keeping a hundred yards behind, we followed into Oxford Street and so down Regent Street. Once our friends stopped and stared into a shop window, which caused Holmes to do the same. An instant afterward he gave a little cry of satisfaction. As I followed the direction of his eager eyes, I saw that a hansom cab with a man inside which had halted on the other side of the street, was now continuing slowly onward again.

"There's our man, Watson! Come along! We'll have a good look at him, if we can do no more."

At that instant I was aware of a bushy black beard and a pair of piercing eyes turned upon us through the side window of the cab. Instantly the trapdoor at the top flew up, something was screamed to the driver, and the cab flew madly off down Regent Street. Holmes looked eagerly around for another, but no empty one was in sight. Then he dashed in wild pursuit amid the stream of the traffic, but the start was too great, and already the cab was out of sight.

"There now!" said Holmes bitterly as he emerged panting and white with irritation from the tide of vehicles. "Was ever such bad luck and such bad management, too? Watson, if you are an honest man you will record this also and set it against my successes!"

"Who was the man?"

"I have no idea."

"A spy?"

"Well, it was clear from what we have heard that Baskerville has been very closely followed by someone since he has been in town. How else could it be known so quickly that it was the Northumberland Hotel which he had chosen? If they had followed him on the first day, I argued that they would follow him also on the second. You may have noticed that I twice strolled over to the window while Dr. Mortimer was reading his legend."

"Yes, I remember."

"I was looking out for people hanging around in the street, but I saw none. We are dealing with a clever man, Watson. This matter cuts very deep, and though I have not yet made up my mind whether it is a good or an evil person who is in touch with us, I am conscious always of power and planning. When our friends left, I at once followed them in the hopes of getting a good look at the person who shadowed them. He was so clever that he did not trust himself to walk, but he hired a cab so that he could linger behind or dash past them and so escape their notice. His method had the additional advantage that if they were to take a cab he was all ready to follow them. It has, however, one obvious disadvantage."

"It puts him in the power of the cabman."

"Exactly."

"What a pity we did not get the number!"

"My dear Watson, clumsy as I have been, you surely do not seriously imagine that I failed to get the number? No. 2704 is our man. But that is no use to us for the moment."

"I fail to see how you could have done more."

"On observing the cab I should have instantly turned and walked in the other direction. I should then at my leisure have hired a second cab and followed the first at a respectful distance, or, better still, have driven to the Northumberland Hotel and waited there. When our unknown had followed Baskerville home, we would have been able to follow him and see where he went. As it is, by our reckless eagerness, which was taken advantage of with amazing quickness and energy by our opponent, we have betrayed ourselves and lost our man."

We had been wandering slowly down Regent Street during this conversation, and Dr. Mortimer, with his companion, had long vanished in front of us.

"There is no longer any reason for our following them," said Holmes. "The shadow has departed and will not return. We must see what other cards we have in our hands and play them boldly. Could you swear to that man's face within the cab?"

"I could swear only to the beard."

"And so could I—from which I gather that it

was probably a false one. A clever man who is involved in something so sensitive has no use for a beard except to hide his features. Come in here, Watson!"

He turned into one of the district messenger offices, where he was warmly greeted by the manager.

"Ah, Wilson, I see you have not forgotten the little case in which I had the good fortune to help you?"

"No, sir, indeed I have not. You saved my good name, and perhaps my life."

"My dear fellow, you exaggerate. I seem to remember, Wilson, that you had among your boys a lad named Cartwright, who showed some ability during the investigation."

"Yes, sir, he is still with us."

"Could you call him?—Thank you! And I would be glad if you would give me change for this five-pound note."

A boy of fourteen, with a bright, keen face, had obeyed the summons of the manager. He stood now gazing worshipfully at the famous detective.

"Let me have the Hotel Directory," said Holmes. "Thank you! Now, Cartwright, there are the names of twenty-three hotels here, all in the immediate neighborhood of Charing Cross. Do you see?"

"Yes, sir."

"You will visit each of these in turn."

"Yes, sir."

"You will begin in each case by giving the doorman one shilling. Here are twenty-three shillings."

"Yes, sir."

"You will tell him that you want to see the wastepaper of yesterday. You will say that an important telegram has become misdirected and that you are looking for it. You understand?"

"Yes, sir."

"But what you are really looking for is the center page of the *Times* with some holes cut in it with scissors. Here is a copy of the *Times*. It is this page. You could easily recognize it, couldn't you?"

"Yes, sir."

"In each case the doorman will send for the hall porter. You will also give him a shilling. Here are twenty-three shillings. You will then learn in possibly twenty cases out of the twenty-three that the waste of the day before has been burned or removed. In the three other cases you will be shown a heap of paper and you will look for this page of the *Times* among it. The odds are enormously against your finding it. There are ten shillings over in case of emergencies. Let me have a report by telegram at my home in Baker Street before evening. And now, Watson, it only remains for us to find out by telegram the identity of the cabman, No. 2704. After that, we will drop into one of the Bond Street art galleries and fill in the time until we are due at the hotel."

CHAPTER 5

Three Broken Threads

Sherlock Holmes had an amazing ability to refocus his attention on other matters. For two hours he appeared to forget about the strange business we had been involved in. Instead, he became totally absorbed in the paintings of the modern Belgian masters. He would talk of nothing but art from the time we left the gallery until we found ourselves at the Northumberland Hotel.

"Sir Henry Baskerville is upstairs expecting you," said the clerk. "He asked me to show you up at once when you came."

"Do you have any objection to my looking at your register?" said Holmes.

"Not in the least."

The book showed that two names had been added after that of Baskerville. One was Theophilus Johnson and family, of Newcastle; the other Mrs. Oldmore and maid, of High Lodge, Alton.

"Surely that must be the same Johnson whom I used to know," said Holmes to the porter. "A lawyer, isn't he, gray-headed, and walks with a limp?"

"No, sir, this is Mr. Johnson, the coal owner, a very active gentleman, no older than yourself."

"Surely you are mistaken about his trade?"

"No, sir! He has used this hotel for many years, and he is very well known to us."

"Ah, that settles it. Mrs. Oldmore, too; I seem to remember the name. Excuse my curiosity, but often in calling upon one friend one finds another."

"She is an invalid lady, sir. Her husband was once mayor of Gloucester. She always comes to us when she is in town."

"Thank you; I am afraid I cannot claim to know her. We have established a most important fact by these questions, Watson," he continued in a low voice as we went upstairs together. "We know now that the people who are so interested in our friend have not settled down in his own hotel. That means that while they are very eager to watch him, they are equally eager that he should not see them. Now, this is a most suggestive fact."

"What does it suggest?"

"It suggests—hello, my dear fellow, what on earth is the matter?"

As we came around the top of the stairs, we

ran up against Sir Henry Baskerville himself. His face was flushed with anger, and he held an old and dusty boot in one of his hands. He was so angry that he could hardly speak, and when he did speak it was with a much broader and more Western slang than any which we had heard from him in the morning.

"Seems to me they are playing me for a sucker in this hotel," he cried. "They'll find they've started in to monkey with the wrong man unless they are careful. By thunder, if that chap can't find my missing boot, there will be trouble. I can take a joke with the best, Mr. Holmes, but they've gone too far this time."

"Still looking for your boot?"

"Yes, sir, and mean to find it."

"But, surely, you said that it was a new brown boot?"

"So it was, sir. And now it's an old black one."

"What! You don't mean to say?"

"That's just what I do mean to say. I only had three pairs in the world—the new brown, the old black, and the patent leathers, which I am wearing. Last night they took one of my brown ones, and today they have sneaked one of the black. Well, have you got it? Speak out, man, and don't stand staring!"

An excited German waiter had appeared upon the scene.

"No, sir, I have asked all over the hotel, but no one knows anything about it."

"Well, either that boot comes back before sundown or I'll see the manager and tell him that I go right straight out of this hotel."

"It shall be found, sir—I promise you that if you will have a little patience it will be found."

"See that it is, for it's the last thing of mine that I'll lose in this den of thieves. Well, well, Mr. Holmes, you'll excuse my troubling you about such a trifle—"

"I think it's well worth troubling about."

"Why, you look very serious over it."

"How do you explain it?"

"I just don't try to explain it. It seems like the craziest, strangest thing that ever happened to me."

"The strangest perhaps—" said Holmes thoughtfully.

"What do you make of it yourself?"

"Well, I don't claim to understand it yet. This case of yours is very complex, Sir Henry. When taken together with your uncle's death, I am not sure that of all the hundreds of major cases which I have handled there is one which cuts so deep. But we hold several threads in our hands, and the odds are that one or other of them guides us to the truth. We may waste time in following the wrong one, but sooner or later we must come upon the right."

We had a pleasant luncheon, during which we didn't speak much of the business which had brought us together. It was in the private sitting room that we went to after lunch that Holmes asked Baskerville what he had decided to do.

"To go to Baskerville Hall."

"And when?"

"At the end of the week."

"On the whole," said Holmes, "I think that your decision is a wise one. I have much evidence that you are being followed in London, and amid the millions of people in this great city it is difficult to discover who these people are or what their motive can be. If their purpose is evil they might do you harm, and we would be powerless to prevent it. You did not know, Dr. Mortimer, that you were followed this morning from my house?"

Dr. Mortimer started violently.

"Followed! By whom?"

"That, unfortunately, is what I cannot tell you. Do you have among your neighbors or acquaintances on Dartmoor any man with a black, full beard?"

"No—or, let me see—why, yes. Barrymore, Sir Charles's butler, is a man with a full, black beard."

"Ha! Where is Barrymore?"

"He is in charge of the Hall."

"We had best learn if he is really there, or if

he might possibly be in London."

"How can you do that?"

"Give me a telegraph form. 'Is all ready for Sir Henry?' That will do. Address to Mr. Barrymore, Baskerville Hall. What is the nearest telegraph office? Grimpen. Very good, we will send a second message to the postmaster, Grimpen: 'Telegram to Mr. Barrymore to be delivered into his own hand. If absent, please return message to Sir Henry Baskerville, Northumberland Hotel.' That should let us know before evening whether Barrymore is at his post in Devonshire or not."

"That's so," said Baskerville. "By the way, Dr. Mortimer, who is this Barrymore, anyhow?"

"He is the son of the old caretaker, who is dead. They have looked after the Hall for four generations now. So far as I know, he and his wife are as respectable a couple as any in the county."

"At the same time," said Baskerville, "it's clear enough that so long as there are none of the family at the Hall, these people have a mighty fine home and nothing to do."

"That is true."

"Did Barrymore profit at all by Sir Charles's will?" asked Holmes.

"He and his wife received five hundred pounds each."

"Ha! Did they know that they would receive this?"

"Yes; Sir Charles was very fond of talking about who he was going to leave money to."

"That is very interesting."

"I hope," said Dr. Mortimer, "that you do not look with suspicious eyes upon everyone who received an inheritance from Sir Charles, for I also had a thousand pounds left to me."

"Indeed! And anyone else?"

"There were many small sums to individuals, and a large number of public charities. The remainder all went to Sir Henry."

"And how much was the remainder?"

"Seven hundred and forty thousand pounds."

Holmes raised his eyebrows in surprise. "I had no idea that so gigantic an amount was involved," said he.

"Sir Charles had the reputation of being rich, but we did not know how very rich he was until we came to examine his financial holdings. The total value of the estate was close on to a million."

"Dear me! It is a prize for which a man might well play a desperate game. And one more question, Dr. Mortimer. Supposing that anything happened to our young friend here—you will forgive the unpleasant suggestion!—who would inherit the estate?"

"Since Rodger Baskerville, Sir Charles's younger brother died unmarried, the estate would descend to the Desmonds, who are distant cousins. James Desmond is an elderly minister in Westmoreland."

"Thank you. These details are all of great interest. Have you met Mr. James Desmond?"

"Yes; he once came down to visit Sir Charles. He is a man of very respectable appearance who has led a saintly life. I remember that he refused to accept any money from Sir Charles, though he pressed it upon him."

"And this man of simple tastes would be the heir to Sir Charles's thousands."

"He would be the heir to the estate because that is what the law requires. He would also be the heir to the money unless the present owner willed it to someone else."

"And have you made your will, Sir Henry?"

"No, Mr. Holmes, I have not. I've had no time, for it was only yesterday that I learned how matters stood. But in any case, I feel that the money should go with the title and estate. That was my poor uncle's idea. How is the owner going to restore the glories of the Baskervilles if he doesn't have enough money to keep up the property? House, land, and dollars must go together."

"Quite so. Well, Sir Henry, I agree that you should go to Devonshire without delay. There is only one recommendation which I must make. You certainly must not go alone."

"Dr. Mortimer returns with me."

"But Dr. Mortimer has his practice to attend to, and his house is miles away from yours. With all the good will in the world, he may be unable to help you. No, Sir Henry, you must take with you someone, a trusty man, who will be always by your side."

"Is it possible that you could come yourself, Mr. Holmes?"

"If matters came to a crisis I would try to be present in person. You can understand, however, that, with my large consulting practice and with the constant appeals which reach me from many places, it is impossible for me to be absent from London for an indefinite time. At the present time, one of the most honored names in England is being muddied by a blackmailer, and only I can stop a disastrous scandal. You see how impossible it is for me to go to Dartmoor."

"Whom would you recommend, then?"

Holmes laid his hand upon my arm.

"If my friend would undertake it, there is no man who is better worth having at your side when you are in a tight place. No one can say so more confidently than I."

The suggestion took me completely by surprise, but before I had time to answer, Baskerville seized me by the hand and shook it heartily.

"Well, now, that is real kind of you, Dr. Watson," said he. "You see how it is with me, and you know just as much about the matter as I do. If you will come down to Baskerville Hall and see me through, I'll never forget it."

The promise of adventure had always fascinated me, and I was flattered by the words of Holmes and by the eagerness with which the baronet greeted me as a companion.

"I will come, with pleasure," said I. "I do not know how I could use my time better."

"And you will report very carefully to me," said Holmes. "When a crisis comes, as it will do, I will direct how you shall act. I suppose you might be ready by Saturday?"

"Would that suit Dr. Watson?"

"Perfectly."

"Then on Saturday, unless you hear differently, we shall meet at the ten-thirty train from Paddington."

We had risen to depart when Baskerville gave a cry of triumph, and diving into one of the corners of the room, he drew a brown boot from under a cabinet.

"My missing boot!" he cried.

"May all our difficulties vanish as easily!" said Sherlock Holmes.

"But it is a very, odd thing," Dr. Mortimer remarked. "I searched this room carefully before lunch."

"And so did I," said Baskerville. "Every inch of it."

"There was certainly no boot in it then."

"In that case, the waiter must have placed it there while we were eating lunch."

The German was sent for but claimed to know nothing of the matter. Nor could any questioning clear it up. Another item had been added to our chain of small mysteries. Setting aside the whole grim story of Sir Charles's death, we had a line of unexplained incidents all within the space of two days. These incidents included the receipt of the printed letter, the black-bearded spy in the hansom, the loss of the new brown boot, the loss of the old black boot, and now the return of the new brown boot. Holmes sat in silence in the cab as we drove back to Baker Street. I knew from his knit eyebrows and alert face that his mind was busy trying to fit all these strange and seemingly disconnected incidents into some kind of pattern. All afternoon and late into the evening he sat lost in tobacco and thought.

Just before dinner two telegrams were handed in. The first ran:

> Have just heard that Barrymore is at the Hall.
>
> BASKERVILLE

The second:

> Visited twenty-three hotels as directed, but sorry to report unable to trace cut sheet of Times.
>
> CARTWRIGHT

"There go two of my threads, Watson. There is nothing more exciting than a case where everything goes against you. We must search around for another scent."

"We still have the cabman who drove the spy."

"Exactly. I have telegraphed to get his name and address from the Official Registry. I would not be surprised if this were an answer to my question."

The ring at the bell proved to be something even better than an answer, however, for the door opened and a rough-looking fellow entered who seemed to be the man himself.

"I got a message from the head office that a gent at this address had been asking for No. 2704," said he. "I've driven my cab for seven years and never had a word of complaint. I came here straight from the Yard to ask you to your face what you had against me."

"I have nothing in the world against you, my good man," said Holmes. "Quite the opposite, I have half a sovereign for you if you will give me a clear answer to my questions."

"Well, I've had a good day and no mistake," said the cabman with a grin. "What was it you wanted to ask, sir?"

"First of all your name and address, in case I want you again."

"John Clayton, 3 Turpey Street, the Borough.

My cab is out of Shipley's Yard, near Waterloo Station."

Sherlock Holmes made a note of it.

"Now, Clayton, tell me all about your passenger who came and watched this house at ten o'clock this morning and afterward followed the two gentlemen down Regent Street."

The man looked surprised and a little embarrassed. "Why there's no good my telling you things, for you seem to know as much as I do already," said he. "The truth is that the gentleman told me that he was a detective and that I was to say nothing about him to anyone."

"My good fellow; this is a very serious business, and you may find yourself in a pretty bad position if you try to hide anything from me. You say that your passenger told you that he was a detective?"

"Yes, he did."

"When did he say this?"

"When he left me."

"Did he say anything more?"

"He mentioned his name."

Holmes cast a swift glance of triumph at me. "Oh, he mentioned his name, did he? That was foolish. What was the name that he mentioned?"

"His name," said the cabman "was Mr. Sherlock Holmes."

Never have I seen my friend more completely taken aback than by the cabman's reply. For an instant he sat in silent amazement. Then he burst into a hearty laugh.

"A hit, Watson—a definite hit!" said he. "I feel a sword as fast and sharp as my own. He got me very nicely that time. So his name was Sherlock Holmes, was it?"

"Yes, sir, that was the gentleman's name."

"Excellent! Tell me where you picked him up and all that occurred."

"He hailed me at half-past nine in Trafalgar Square. He said that he was a detective, and he offered me two guineas if I would do exactly what he wanted all day and ask no questions. I was glad enough to agree. First we drove down to the Northumberland Hotel and waited there until two gentlemen came out and took a cab from the cab stand. We followed their cab until it pulled up somewhere near here."

"This very door," said Holmes.

"Well, I couldn't be sure of that, but I dare say my passenger knew all about it. We pulled up halfway down the street and waited an hour and a half. Then the two gentlemen passed us, walking, and we followed down Baker Street and along—"

"I know," said Holmes.

"Until we got three-quarters down Regent Street. Then my gentleman opened the little door on the top of the cab, and he shouted that I should drive right away to Waterloo Station as hard as I could go. I whipped up the mare and we were there in less than ten minutes. Then he paid up his two guineas, like a good one, and away he went into the station. Only just as he was leaving he turned around and he said: 'It might interest you to know that you have been driving Mr. Sherlock Holmes.' That's how I come to know the name."

"I see. And you saw no more of him?"

"Not after he went into the station."

"And how would you describe Mr. Sherlock Holmes?"

The cabman scratched his head. "Well, he wasn't altogether such an easy gentleman to describe. I'd put him at forty years of age, and he was of a middle height, two or three inches shorter than you, sir. He was dressed like a dandy, and he had a black beard, cut square at the end, and a pale face. I don't know as I could say more than that."

"Color of his eyes?"

"No, I can't say that."

"Nothing more that you can remember?"

"No sir, nothing."

"Well, then, here is your half-sovereign. There's another one waiting for you if you can bring any more information. Good night!"

"Good night, sir, and thank you!"

John Clayton departed chuckling, and Holmes turned to me with a shrug of his shoulders and a sad smile.

"Snap goes our third thread, and we end where we began," said he. "The clever rascal! He knew our number, knew that Sir Henry Baskerville had asked for my advice, spotted who I was in Regent Street, guessed that I had gotten the number of the cab and would lay my hands on the driver, and so sent back this impudent message. I tell you, Watson, this time we have an enemy who is worthy of our steel. I've been checkmated in London. I can only wish you better luck in Devonshire. But I don't feel confident about it."

"About what?"

"About sending you. It's an ugly business, Watson, an ugly dangerous business, and the more I see of it the less I like it. Yes my dear fellow, you may laugh, but I give you my word that I shall be very glad to have you back safe and sound in Baker Street once more."

CHAPTER 6

Baskerville Hall

Sir Henry Baskerville and Dr. Mortimer were ready on Saturday, and we started as planned for Devonshire. Mr. Sherlock Holmes drove with me to the station and gave me his last parting warnings and advice.

"I will not prejudice you by suggesting theories or suspicions, Watson," said he. "I wish you simply to report facts in the fullest possible manner to me. You can leave me to do the theorizing."

"What sort of facts?" I asked.

"Anything which may seem to have some connection to the case, and especially the relations between young Baskerville and his neighbors or any fresh facts concerning the death of Sir Charles. I have done some checking myself in the last few days, but the results have, I fear, been negative. One thing only appears to be certain, and that is that Mr. James Desmond, who is the next heir, is an elderly gentleman with a kind heart. He is evidently not responsible for this targeting of the Baskervilles. I really think that we may cross him off our list. There remain the people who will actually surround Sir Henry Baskerville out on the moor."

"Shouldn't we, in the first place, get rid of this Barrymore couple?"

"By no means. You could not make a greater mistake. If they are innocent it would be a cruel injustice, and if they are guilty we would be giving up all chance of catching them in the act. No, no, we will keep them on our list of suspects. Then there is a groom at the Hall, if I remember right. There are two moorland farmers. There is our friend Dr. Mortimer, whom I believe is entirely honest, and there is his wife, of whom we know nothing. There is this naturalist, Stapleton, and there is his sister, who is said to be an attractive young lady. There is Mr. Frankland, of Lafter Hall, who is also an unknown factor, and there are one or two other neighbors. These are the people who you must pay close attention to."

"I will do my best."

"You have weapons, I suppose?"

"Yes, I thought I had better take them."

"Most certainly. Keep your revolver near you night and day, and never relax your guard."

Our friends had already paid for a first-class train compartment and were waiting for us on the platform.

"No, we have no news of any kind," said Dr. Mortimer in answer to my friend's questions. "I can swear to one thing, and that is that we have not been followed during the last two days. We have never gone out without keeping a sharp watch, and no one could have escaped our notice."

"You have always stayed together, I hope?"

"Except yesterday afternoon. I usually allow myself one day of pleasure when I come to town, so I spent it at the Museum of the College of Surgeons."

"And I went to look at the people in the park," said Baskerville. "But we had no trouble of any kind."

"It was unwise, all the same," said Holmes, shaking his head and looking very serious. "I beg, Sir Henry, that you will not walk around alone. Some great misfortune will befall you if you do. Did you get your other boot?"

"No, sir, it is gone forever."

"Indeed. That is very interesting. Well, goodbye," he added as the train began to glide down the platform. "Keep in mind, Sir Henry, one of the phrases in that strange old legend which Dr. Mortimer has read to us and avoid the moor late at night when the powers of evil are at their height."

I looked back at the platform when we had left it far behind and saw the tall, thin figure of

Holmes standing motionless and gazing after us.

The journey was a swift and pleasant one. I spent it in getting to know my two companions and in playing with Dr. Mortimer's spaniel. In a very few hours the brown earth had become reddish, the brick had changed to granite, and red cows grazed in well-hedged fields where the lush grasses and vegetation told of a richer and wetter climate. Young Baskerville stared eagerly out of the window and cried aloud with delight as he recognized the familiar features of the Devon scenery.

"I've been over much of the world since I left it, Dr. Watson," said he, "but I have never seen a place to compare with it."

"I never saw a Devonshire man who did not swear by his county," I remarked.

"It depends upon the breed of men quite as much as on the county," said Dr. Mortimer. "A glance at our friend here reveals the rounded head of the Celt, which carries inside it the Celtic enthusiasm and tendency to get attached to things. Poor Sir Charles's head was of a very rare type, half Gaelic, half Ivernian. But you were very young when you last saw Baskerville Hall, weren't you?"

"I was a boy in my teens at the time of my father's death and had never seen the Hall, for he lived in a little cottage on the South Coast. From there I went straight to a friend in America. I tell you it is all as new to me as it is to Dr. Watson, and I'm as eager as possible to see the moor."

"Are you? Then your wish is easily granted, for there is your first sight of the moor," said Dr. Mortimer, pointing out of the train window.

Over the green squares of the fields and the low curve of a forest, there rose in the distance a gray, sad-looking hill, with a strange jagged summit, dim and hazy in the distance, like some fantastic landscape in a dream. Baskerville sat for a long time with his eyes fixed upon it. As I looked at him, I read upon his eager face how much it meant to him, this first sight of that strange spot where his ancestors had held power so long and left their mark so deep. There he sat, with his tweed suit and his American accent, in the corner of an ordinary railway car. And yet as I looked at his dark and expressive face, I felt more than ever how true a descendant he was of that long line of high-blooded, fiery, and masterful men. There were pride, courage, and strength in his thick brows, his sensitive nostrils, and his large hazel eyes. If a dangerous adventure should lie before us on that forbidding moor, I had confidence that he would be willing to bravely share any risk.

The train pulled up at a small wayside station and we all stepped down. Outside, beyond the low, white fence, a small wagon with a pair of sturdy horses was waiting. Our coming was evidently a great event, for stationmaster and porters clustered around us to carry out our luggage. It was a sweet, simple country spot, but I was surprised to see two soldierly men in dark uniforms who stood by a gate, leaned upon their short rifles, and glanced with interest at us as we passed. The coachman, a hard faced, weather-beaten little fellow, saluted Sir Henry Baskerville, and in a few minutes we were flying swiftly down the broad, white road. Rolling pasture lands curved upward on either side of us, and old houses with peaked roofs peeped out from amid the thick green foliage. But behind the peaceful and sunlit countryside there rose as always, dark against the evening sky, the long, gloomy curve of the moor, broken by the jagged and cruel-looking hills.

The little wagon swung around into a side road, and we curved upward through deep lanes worn by centuries of wheels, high banks on either side, heavy with dripping moss and fleshy ferns. Bronzing ferns and spotted bushes gleamed in the light of the sinking sun. Still steadily rising, we passed over a narrow granite bridge and rode beside a noisy stream which gushed swiftly down, foaming and roaring amid the gray boulders. Both road and stream wound up through a valley dense with scrub oak and fir. At every turn Baskerville gave an exclamation of delight, looking eagerly about him and asking countless questions. To his eyes all seemed beautiful, but to me a tinge of sorrow lay upon the countryside, which bore so clearly the mark of autumn decay. Yellow leaves carpeted the lanes and fluttered down upon us as we passed. The rattle of our wheels died away as we drove through drifts of rotting vegetation—sad gifts, as it seemed to me, for Nature to throw before the carriage of the returning heir of the Baskervilles.

"Hello!" cried Dr. Mortimer, "what is this?"

A steep curve of heath-clad land, an outlying spur of the moor lay in front of us. On the summit, hard and clear like a statue of a horse and rider upon its stand, was a mounted soldier, dark and stern, his rifle poised ready over his forearm. He was watching the road along which we traveled.

"What is this, Perkins?" asked Dr. Mortimer.

Our driver half turned in his seat.

"There's a convict escaped from Princetown, sir. He's been out three days now, and the guards watch every road and every station, but they've had no sight of him yet. The farmers about here don't like it, sir, and that's a fact."

"Well, I understand that they get five pounds if they can give information."

"Yes, sir, but the chance of five pounds is but a poor thing compared to the chance of having your throat cut. You see, it isn't like any ordinary convict. This is a man that would stop at nothing."

"Who is he, then?"

"It is Selden, the Notting Hill murderer."

I remembered the case well, for it was one which had interested Holmes on account of the strange viciousness of the crime and the reckless brutality of all the murderer's actions. The reduction of his death sentence to life imprisonment had been due to the fact that people doubted his sanity, so horrible was his conduct. Our wagon had gotten to the top of a hill. In front of us rose the huge expanse of the moor, spotted with twisted and craggy piles of stone and high rocks. A cold wind swept down from it and set us shivering. Somewhere out on that lonely plain, this devilish man was lurking, hiding in a burrow like a wild beast, his heart full of cruel revenge against the whole race which had cast him out. Imagining his presence only added to the grim reality of the barren waste, the chilling wind, and the darkening sky. Even Baskerville fell silent and pulled his overcoat more closely around him.

We had left the fertile country behind and beneath us. We looked back on it now, the slanting rays of a low sun turning the streams to threads of gold and glowing on the newly plowed earth and the broad tangle of the woodlands. The road in front of us grew bleaker and wilder over huge reddish and olive slopes, sprinkled with giant boulders. Now and then we passed a moorland cottage, walled and roofed with stone, with no ivy to break its harsh outline. Suddenly we looked down into a cuplike valley, patched with stunted oaks and firs which had been twisted and bent by the fury of years of storm. Two high, narrow towers rose over the trees. The driver pointed with his whip.

"Baskerville Hall," said he.

Its master had risen and was staring with flushed cheeks and shining eyes. A few minutes later we had reached the lodge gates, a maze of fantastic grillwork in wrought iron, with weather-bitten pillars on either side, discolored by tiny parasitic plants, and topped by the boars' heads of the Baskervilles. The lodge was a ruin of black granite and bared ribs of rafters. Facing it, however, was a new building, half constructed, the first fruit of Sir Charles's South African gold.

Through the gateway we passed into the avenue, where the wheels were again hushed amid the leaves, and the old trees shot their branches in a gloomy tunnel over our heads. Baskerville shuddered as he looked up the long, dark drive to where the house glimmered like a ghost at the farther end.

"Was it here?" he asked in a low voice.

"No, no, the yew alley is on the other side."

The young heir glanced around with a gloomy face.

"It's no wonder my uncle felt as if trouble were coming on him in such a place as this," said he. "It's enough to scare any man. I'll put a row of electric lights up here inside of six months, and you won't know it again, with a thousand watts of power right here in front of the hall door."

The avenue opened into a broad expanse of grass, and the house lay before us. In the fading light I could see that the center was a heavy block of building from which a porch projected. The whole front was draped in ivy, with a patch clipped bare here and there where a window or a coat of arms broke through the dark veil. From this central block rose the twin towers, ancient, notched with battlements, and pierced with many holes that one could shoot a gun through. To the right and left of the towers were more modern wings of black granite. A dull light shone through heavy windows. A single, black column of smoke sprang from the high chimneys which rose from the steep, high-angled roof.

"Welcome, Sir Henry! Welcome to Baskerville Hall!"

A tall man had stepped from the shadow of the porch to open the door of the wagon. The figure of a woman was outlined against the yellow light of the hall. She came out and helped the man hand down our bags.

"You don't mind my driving straight home, Sir Henry?" said Dr. Mortimer. "My wife is expecting me."

"Surely you will stay and have some dinner?"

"No, I must go. I shall probably find some work awaiting me. I would stay to show you over the house, but Barrymore will be a better guide than I. Goodbye, and never hesitate night or day to send for me if I can be of service."

The wheels died away down the drive while Sir Henry and I turned into the hall, and the door clanged heavily behind us. It was a fine room in which we found ourselves, large, lofty, and strongly supported with huge beams of age-blackened oak. In the great old-fashioned fireplace behind the high iron dogs, a log fire crackled and snapped. Sir Henry and I held out our hands to it, for we were numb from our long drive. Then we gazed around us at the high, thin window of old stained glass, the oak paneling, the stags' heads, and the coats of arms upon the walls. All were dim and gloomy in the weak light of the central lamp.

"It's just as I imagined it," said Sir Henry. "Is it not the very picture of an old family home? To think that this should be the same hall in which my people lived for five hundred years. It strikes me speechless to think about it."

I saw his dark face lit up with a boyish enthusiasm as he gazed about him. The light beat upon him where he stood, but long shadows trailed down the walls and hung like a black canopy above him. Barrymore had returned from taking our luggage to our rooms. He stood in front of us now with the quiet and respectful manner of a well-trained servant. He was a remarkable-looking man, tall, handsome, with a square black beard and pale, distinguished features.

"Would you wish dinner to be served at once, sir?"

"Is it ready?"

"In a very few minutes, sir. You will find hot water in your rooms. My wife and I will be happy, Sir Henry, to stay with you until you have made fresh arrangements, but you will understand that under the new conditions this house will require a much larger staff."

"What new conditions?"

"I only meant, sir, that Sir Charles led a very quiet life, and we were able to look after his wants. You would, naturally, wish to have more company, and so you will need changes in your household."

"Do you mean that your wife and you wish to leave?"

"Only when it is quite convenient to you, sir."

"But your family have been with us for several generations, have they not? I would be sorry to begin my life here by breaking an old family connection."

I seemed to notice some signs of emotion upon the butler's white face.

"I feel that also, sir, and so does my wife. But to tell the truth, sir, we were both very attached to Sir Charles and his death gave us a shock and made these surroundings very painful to us. I fear that we shall never again be at ease at Baskerville Hall."

"But what do you plan to do?"

"I have no doubt, sir, that we shall succeed in establishing ourselves in some business. Sir Charles's generosity has given us the means to do so. And now, sir, perhaps I had best show you to your rooms."

A square hall bordered by a railing ran around the top of the old house and was approached by a double stair. From this central point, two long hallways extended the whole length of the building. All the bedrooms opened onto these hallways. My own was in the same wing as Baskerville's and almost next door to it. These rooms appeared to be much more modern than the central part of the house, and the bright wallpaper and many candles did something to remove the gloomy impression which our arrival had left upon my mind.

But the dining room which opened out of the hall was a place of shadow and gloom. It was a long chamber with a step separating the raised area where the family sat from the lower portion reserved for their dependents. A musician's gallery overlooked it on one end. Black beams shot across above our heads, with a smoke-darkened ceiling beyond them. With rows of flaring torches to light it up, and the color and crude hilarity of an old-time banquet, it might have softened. Now, however, when two black-clothed gentlemen sat in the little circle of light thrown by a shaded lamp, one's voice became hushed and one's spirit subdued. A dim line of ancestors, in every variety of dress, from knights to fancy gentlemen, stared down upon us and spooked us by their silent company. We didn't talk much, and I was glad when the meal was over and we were able to retire into the modern billiard room and smoke a cigarette.

"My word, it isn't a very cheerful place," said Sir Henry. "I suppose one can adjust to it, but I feel a bit out-of-place right now. I don't wonder that my uncle got a little jumpy when he lived here all alone. However, if it suits you, we will retire early tonight, and perhaps things may seem more cheerful in the morning."

I drew aside my curtains before I went to bed and looked out from my window. It opened upon the grassy space which lay in front of the hall door. Beyond, two thickets of trees moaned and swung in a rising wind. A half moon broke through the racing clouds. In its cold light, I saw beyond the trees a broken fringe of rocks, and the long, low curve of the dreary moor. I closed the curtain, feeling that my last impression was in keeping with the rest.

And yet it was not quite the last. I found myself tired and yet wakeful, tossing restlessly from side to side, seeking for the sleep which would not come. Far away a chiming clock struck each quarter-hour, but otherwise a deathly silence lay upon the old house. And then suddenly, in the very dead of the night, there came a sound to my ears, clear, loud, and unmistakable. It was the sob of a woman, the muffled, strangling gasp of one who is torn by an uncontrollable sorrow. I sat up in bed and listened intently. The noise could not have been far away and was certainly in the house. For half an hour I waited with every nerve on the alert, but there came no other sound save the chiming clock and the rustle of the ivy on the wall.

CHAPTER 7

The Stapletons of Merripit House

The fresh beauty of the following morning did something to erase from our minds the grim and gray impression which our first experience of Baskerville Hall had given us. As Sir Henry and I sat at breakfast, the sunlight flooded in through the high windows, throwing watery patches of color from the coats of arms which covered them. The dark paneling glowed like bronze in the golden rays, and it was hard to realize that this was indeed the room which had struck such a gloom into our souls the evening before.

"I guess we should blame ourselves and not the house!" said the baronet. "We were tired by our journey and chilled by our drive, so we took a dim view of the place. Now we are fresh and well, so it is all cheerful once more."

"And yet it was not entirely a question of imagination," I answered. "Did you, for example, happen to hear someone, a woman I think, sobbing in the night?"

"That is odd, for I did when I was half asleep imagine that I heard something of the sort. I waited quite a while, but there was no more of it, so I decided that it was all a dream."

"I heard it clearly, and I am sure that it was really the sob of a woman."

"We must ask about this right away." He rang the bell and asked Barrymore whether he could give an explanation for our experience. It seemed to me that the pallid features of the butler turned a shade paler as he listened to his master's question.

"There are only two women in the house, Sir Henry," he answered. "One is the kitchen maid, who sleeps in the other wing. The other is my wife, and I can answer for it that the sound could not have come from her."

And yet he lied as he said it, for it chanced that after breakfast I met Mrs. Barrymore in the long corridor with the sun full upon her face. She was a large, heavy-set woman with a stern mouth. But her telltale eyes were red and glanced at me from between swollen lids. It was she, then, who wept in the night, and if she did so, her husband must know it. Yet he had taken the obvious risk of discovery in stating that it was not so. Why had he done this? And why did she weep so bitterly? Already around this pale-faced, handsome, black-bearded man there was gathering an atmosphere of mystery and of gloom. It was he who had been the first to discover the body of Sir Charles, and we had only his word for all the circumstances which led up to the old man's death. Was it possible that it was Barrymore, after all, whom we had seen in the cab in Regent Street? The beard might well have been the same. The cabman had described a somewhat shorter man, but such an impression might easily have been mistaken. How could I settle the question once and for all? Obviously the first thing to do was to see the Grimpen postmaster and find whether the test telegram had really been placed in Barrymore's own hands. Whatever his answer, I would at least have something to report to Sherlock Holmes.

Sir Henry had many papers to look over after breakfast, so that was a good time for me to take my morning walk. It was a pleasant walk of four miles along the edge of the moor, leading me at last to a small gray village, in which two larger buildings, which proved to be the inn and the house of Dr. Mortimer, stood high above the rest. The postmaster, who was also the village grocer, had a clear memory of the telegram.

"Certainly, sir," said he, "I had the telegram delivered to Mr. Barrymore exactly as directed."

"Who delivered it?"

"My boy here. James, you delivered that telegram to Mr. Barrymore at the Hall last week, didn't you?"

"Yes, father, I delivered it."

"Into his own hands?" I asked.

"Well, he was up in the loft at the time, so that I could not put it into his own hands, but I gave it to Mrs. Barrymore, and she promised to deliver it at once."

"Did you see Mr. Barrymore?"

"No, sir; I tell you he was in the loft."

"If you didn't see him, how do you know he was in the loft?"

"Well, surely his own wife ought to know where he is," said the postmaster, beginning to get annoyed. "Didn't he get the telegram? If there is any mistake it is for Mr. Barrymore himself to complain."

It seemed hopeless to question him any longer, but it was clear that in spite of Holmes's strategy, we had no proof that Barrymore had not been in London all the time. Suppose that it were so—suppose that the same man had been the last to see Sir Charles alive, and the first to dog the new heir when he returned to England. What then? Was he the agent of others or did he have some evil goal of his own? What interest could he have in harming the Baskerville family? I thought of the strange warning clipped out of the leading article of the *Times*. Was that his work or was it possibly the doing of someone who was trying to hinder his schemes? The only imaginable motive was that which had been suggested by Sir Henry: that if the family could be scared away a comfortable and permanent home would be secured for the Barrymores. But surely such an explanation as that would not be enough to account for the deep and clever scheming which seemed to be weaving an invisible net around the young baronet. Holmes himself had said that no more complex case had come to him in all his many sensational investigations. I prayed, as I walked back along the gray, lonely road, that my friend might soon be freed from his other business and be able to come down to take this heavy burden of responsibility from my shoulders.

Suddenly my thoughts were interrupted by the sound of running feet behind me and by a voice which called me by name. I turned, expecting to see Dr. Mortimer, but to my surprise it was a stranger who was pursuing me.

He was a small, slim, clean-shaven, neat-looking man, blond-haired and lean-jawed, between thirty and forty years of age. He was dressed in a gray suit and wore a straw hat. A metal box for nature specimens hung over his shoulder and he carried a green butterfly net in one of his hands.

"You will, I am sure, excuse my boldness, Dr. Watson," said he as he came panting up to where I stood. "Here on the moor we are down-to-earth folk and do not wait for formal introductions. You may possibly have heard my name from our mutual friend, Mortimer. I am

Stapleton, of Merripit House."

"Your net and box would have told me as much," said I, "for I knew that Mr. Stapleton was a naturalist. But how did you know me?"

"I have been calling on Mortimer, and he pointed you out to me from the window of his office as you passed. As our road was the same, I thought that I would overtake you and introduce myself. I trust that Sir Henry is none the worse for his journey?"

"He is very well, thank you."

"We were all rather afraid that after the sad death of Sir Charles the new baronet might refuse to live here. It is asking much of a wealthy man to come down and bury himself in a place of this kind, but I need not tell you that it means a very great deal to the countryside. Sir Henry has, I suppose, no superstitious fears in the matter?"

"I do not believe that he does."

"Of course you know the legend of the demon dog which haunts the family?"

"I have heard it."

"It is amazing how gullible the local people are around here! Many of them are ready to swear that they have seen such a creature out on the moor." He spoke with a smile, but I seemed to read in his eyes that he took the matter more seriously. "The story took a great hold upon the imagination of Sir Charles, and I have no doubt that it led to his tragic end."

"But how?"

"His nerves were so worked up that the appearance of any dog might have had a fatal effect upon his diseased heart. I believe that he really did see something of the kind that last night in the yew alley. I feared that some disaster might happen, for I was very fond of the old man, and I knew that his heart was weak."

"How did you know that?"

"My friend Mortimer told me."

"You think, then, that some dog ran after Sir Charles, and that he died of fright as a result?"

"Have you any better explanation?"

"I have not come to any conclusion."

"Has Mr. Sherlock Holmes?"

The words took away my breath for an instant, but a glance at the calm face and steady eyes of my companion showed that he hadn't meant to startle me.

"It is useless for us to pretend that we do not know you, Dr. Watson," said he. "Your writings about Holmes have reached us here, and you could not celebrate him without being well known yourself. When Mortimer told me your name he could not deny your identity. If you are here, then it follows that Mr. Sherlock Holmes is involving himself in the matter, and I am naturally curious to know what view he may take."

"I am afraid that I cannot answer that question."

"May I ask if he is going to honor us with a visit himself?"

"He cannot leave town at present. He has other cases which demand his attention."

"What a pity! He might throw some light on that which is so dark to us. But as to your own researches, if there is any possible way in which I can be of service to you, I trust that you will tell me. If I had any idea as to the nature of your suspicions or how you intend to investigate the case, I might be able to give you some aid or advice."

"I assure you that I am simply here upon a visit to my friend, Sir Henry, and that I need no help of any kind."

"Excellent!" said Stapleton. "You are perfectly right to be suspicious and careful. I apologize for trying to interfere, and I promise you that I will not mention the matter again."

We had come to a point where a narrow grassy path struck off from the road and wound away across the moor. A steep, boulder-sprinkled hill lay upon the right which had long ago been cut into a granite quarry. The face which was turned toward us formed a dark cliff, with ferns and bushes growing in its cracks. From over a distant hill there floated a gray plume of smoke.

"A short walk along this moor path brings us to Merripit House," said he. "Perhaps you will spare an hour so I may have the pleasure of introducing you to my sister."

My first thought was that I should be by Sir Henry's side. But then I remembered the pile of papers and bills he had been looking through. I was certain that I could not help with those. And Holmes had expressly said that I should study the neighbors upon the moor. I accepted Stapleton's invitation, and we turned together down the path.

"It is a wonderful place, the moor," said he, looking around over the rolling uplands, long green waves of grass, with crests of jagged granite foaming up into fantastic peaks. "You never tire of the moor. You cannot imagine the wonderful secrets which it contains. It is so huge, and so barren, and so mysterious."

"You know it well, then?"

"I have only been here two years. The residents would call me a newcomer. We came shortly after Sir Charles settled. But my interests led me to explore every part of the country around here, and I believe that there are few men who know it better than I do."

"Is it hard to know?"

"Very hard. You see, for example, this great plain to the north here with the strange hills breaking out of it. Do you notice anything remarkable about that?"

"It would be a difficult place to go horseback riding."

"You would naturally think so and the

thought has cost several their lives before now. You notice those bright green spots scattered thickly over it?"

"Yes, they seem more lush than the rest."

Stapleton laughed.

"That is the great Grimpen Mire," said he. "A false step over there means death to man or beast. Only yesterday I saw one of the moor ponies wander into it. He never came out. I saw his head for quite a long time straining out of the bog hole, but the mud sucked him down at last. Even in dry seasons it is dangerous to cross it, but after these autumn rains it is an awful place. And yet I can find my way to the very heart of it and return alive. By George, there is another of those miserable ponies!"

Something brown was rolling and tossing among the green weeds. Then a long, agonized, twisting neck shot upward and a dreadful cry echoed over the moor. It turned me cold with horror, but my companion's nerves seemed to be stronger than mine.

"It's gone!" said he. "The soggy soil has him. Two in two days, and many more, perhaps, for they get in the habit of going there in the dry weather and never know the difference until the mire has them in its clutches. It's a bad place, the great Grimpen Mire."

"And you say you can walk through it?"

"Yes, there are one or two paths which a very

active man can take. I have found them out."

"But why should you wish to go into so horrible a place?"

"Well, you see the hills beyond? They are really islands cut off on all sides by the impassable mire, which has crawled round them in the course of years. That is where the rare plants and the butterflies are, if you have the skill to reach them."

"I shall try my luck some day."

He looked at me with a surprised face.

"For God's sake don't think of such a thing," said he. "Your blood would be upon my head. I assure you that there would not be the least chance of your coming back alive. It is only by remembering certain complex landmarks that I am able to do it."

"Hello!" I cried. "What is that?"

A long, low moan, awfully sad, swept over the moor. It filled the whole air, and yet it was impossible to say where it came from. From a dull murmur it swelled into a deep roar. Then it sank back into a sorrowful, throbbing murmur once again. Stapleton looked at me with a curious expression in his face.

"Odd place, the moor!" said he.

"But what is it?"

"The peasants say it is the Hound of the Baskervilles calling for its prey. I've heard it once or twice before, but never quite so loud."

I looked around, with a chill of fear in my heart, at the huge swelling plain, spotted with the green patches of water reeds. Nothing stirred over the vast area except a pair of ravens, which croaked loudly from a high rock behind us.

"You are an educated man. You don't believe such nonsense as that?" said I. "What do you think is the cause of so strange a sound?"

"Bogs make queer noises sometimes. It's the mud settling, or the water rising, or something."

"No, no, that was a living voice."

"Well, perhaps it was. Did you ever hear a bittern booming?"

"No, I never did."

"It's a very rare bird—practically extinct—in England now, but all things are possible upon the moor. Yes, I should not be surprised to learn that what we have heard is the cry of the last of the bitterns."

"It's the weirdest, strangest thing that ever I heard in my life."

"Yes, it's rather an incredible place. Look at the hillside over there. What do you make of those?"

The whole steep slope was covered with round gray rings of stone, twenty of them at least.

"What are they? Sheep pens?"

"No, they are the homes of our worthy ancestors. Prehistoric man lived on the moor, and as very few people have lived there ever since, we find all his little arrangements exactly as he left them. These are his stone huts with the roofs off. You can even see his fireplace and his couch if you're curious enough to go inside.

"But it is quite a town. When was it inhabited?"

"Prehistoric man—no date."

"What did he do?"

"He grazed his cattle on these slopes, and he learned to dig for tin when the bronze sword began to take the place of the stone axe. Look at the great trench in the opposite hill. That is his mark. Yes, you will find some very interesting points about the moor, Dr. Watson. Oh, excuse me an instant! It is surely Cyclopides."

A small fly or moth had fluttered across our path, and in an instant Stapleton was rushing after it with amazing energy and speed. To my dismay the creature flew straight for the great mire. My acquaintance never paused for an instant, but jumped from tuft to tuft behind it, his green net waving in the air. His gray clothes and his jerky, zigzag, irregular progress made him resemble some huge moth himself. I was watching him with a mixture of admiration for his energy and fear that he might lose his footing in the deadly mire when I heard the sound of steps behind me. Turning around, I found a woman near me upon the path. She had come from the direction of Merripit House, but the dip of the moor had hid her until she was quite close.

I did not doubt that this was the Miss Stapleton whom I had heard of, since there were few ladies of any sort on the moor, and I remembered that I had heard her described as being beautiful. The woman who approached me was certainly that, and of a most uncommon type. There could not have been a greater contrast between brother and sister. Whereas Stapleton had a fair complexion, with light hair and gray eyes, she was darker than any brunette whom I have seen in England—slim, elegant, and tall. She had a proud, finely-shaped face, so regular that it might have seemed to lack expression were it not for the sensitive mouth and the beautiful dark, eager eyes. With her perfect figure and elegant dress she was, indeed, a strange vision upon a lonely moorland path. Her eyes were on her brother as I turned, and then she quickened her pace toward me. I had raised my hat and was about to introduce myself when she spoke first and startled me with what she said.

"Go back!" she said. "Go straight back to London, instantly."

I could only stare at her in stupid surprise. Her eyes blazed at me, and she tapped the ground impatiently with her foot.

"Why should I go back?" I asked.

"I cannot explain." She spoke in a low, eager

voice, with a slight lisp. "But for God's sake do what I ask you. Go back and never set foot upon the moor again."

"But I have only just come."

"Man, man!" she cried. "Can you not tell when a warning is for your own good? Go back to London! Start tonight! Get away from this place at all costs! Hush, my brother is coming! Not a word of what I have said. Would you mind getting that orchid for me among the cattails over there? We are very rich in orchids on the moor, though, of course, you are rather late to see the beauties of the place."

Stapleton had abandoned the chase and came back to us breathing hard and flushed with his efforts.

"Hello, Beryl!" said he, and it seemed to me that the tone of his greeting was not altogether a friendly one.

"Well, Jack, you are very hot."

"Yes, I was chasing a Cyclopides. He is very rare and seldom found in the late autumn. What a pity that I should have missed him!" He spoke unconcernedly, but his small light eyes glanced repeatedly from the girl to me.

"You have introduced yourselves, I can see."

"Yes. I was telling Sir Henry that it was a little late for him to see the true beauties of the moor."

"Why, who do you think this is?"

"I imagine that it must be Sir Henry Baskerville."

"No, no," said I. "Only a humble commoner, but his friend. My name is Dr. Watson."

A flush of irritation passed over her expressive face. "We have been talking at cross purposes," said she.

"Why, you didn't have much time for talk," her brother remarked with the same questioning eyes.

"I talked as if Dr. Watson were a resident instead of being merely a visitor," said she. "It cannot much matter to him whether it is early or late for the orchids. But you will come on, will you not, and see Merripit House?"

A short walk brought us to it, a bleak moorland house. It had once been the home of some cattle farmer many years ago, but now it had been repaired and turned into a modern dwelling. An orchard surrounded it, but the trees, as is usual upon the moor, were stunted and small, and the effect of the whole place was mean and sad. We were admitted by a strange, wrinkled, rusty-coated old manservant, who seemed well-suited to the house. Inside, however, there were large rooms furnished with an elegance which seemed to reflect a lady's taste. As I looked from their windows at the endless granite-flecked moor rolling unbroken to the farthest horizon, I could only wonder about what could have brought this highly educated man and this beautiful woman to live in such a place.

"Strange spot to choose, is it not?" said he as if in answer to my thought. "And yet we manage to make ourselves fairly happy, don't we, Beryl?"

"Quite happy," said she, but it didn't sound like she meant it.

"I had a school," said Stapleton. "It was in the north country. I found the work to be mechanical and uninteresting, but the privilege of living with youth, of helping to mould those young minds, and of impressing them with one's own character and ideals was very important to me. However, the fates were against us. A serious epidemic broke out in the school and three of the boys died. It never recovered from the blow, and much of the money I had invested was lost. And yet, if it weren't for the loss of the boys' charming companionship, I could rejoice over my own misfortune, since, with my strong tastes for the life sciences, I find an unlimited field of work here. My sister is as devoted to Nature as I am. I'm telling you this, Dr. Watson, because I noticed your expression as you looked over the moor out of our window."

"It certainly did cross my mind that it might be a little boring—less for you, perhaps, than for your sister."

"No, no, I am never bored," said she quickly. "We have books, we have our studies, and we have interesting neighbors. Dr. Mortimer is a most learned man in his own line of work. Poor Sir Charles was also an admirable companion. We knew him well and miss him more than I can tell. Do you think that I should call this afternoon and meet Sir Henry?"

"I am sure that he would be delighted."

"Then perhaps you would mention that I propose to do so. We may in our modest way do something to make things easier for him until he becomes used to his new home. Will you come upstairs, Dr. Watson, and inspect my butterfly collection? I think it is the most complete one in the southwest of England. By the time that you have looked through them, lunch will be almost ready."

But I was eager to get back to Sir Henry. The sadness of the moor, the death of the unfortunate pony, the weird sound which had been connected with the grim legend of the Baskervilles; all these things depressed me. Then on the top of these more or less vague impressions there had come the definite and distinct warning of Miss Stapleton, delivered with such intense seriousness that I could not doubt that some grave and deep reason lay behind it. I turned down the lunch invitation and set off at once upon my return journey, taking the grassy path by which we had come.

It seems, however, that there must have been some short cut for those who knew it, for before I had reached the road I was astounded to see

Miss Stapleton sitting upon a rock by the side of the track. Her face was beautifully flushed with her efforts and she held her hand to her side.

"I have run all the way in order to cut you off, Dr. Watson," said she. "I didn't even have time to put on my hat. I must not stop or my brother may miss me. I wanted to say to you how sorry I am about the stupid mistake I made in thinking that you were Sir Henry. Please forget the words I said, which were not intended for you."

"But I can't forget them, Miss Stapleton," said I. "I am Sir Henry's friend, and his welfare is a very close concern of mine. Tell me why it was that you were so eager that Sir Henry should return to London."

"A woman's whim, Dr. Watson. When you know me better you will understand that I cannot always give reasons for what I say or do."

"No, no. I remember the excitement in your voice. I remember the look in your eyes. Please, please, be sincere with me, Miss Stapleton, for ever since I have been here I have been aware of shadows all around me. Life has become like that great Grimpen Mire, with little green patches everywhere into which one may sink and with no guide to point out the correct path. Tell me then what it was that you meant, and I will promise to give your warning to Sir Henry."

A look of indecision passed for an instant

over her face, but her eyes had hardened again when she answered me.

"You make too much of it, Dr. Watson," said she. "My brother and I were very much shocked by the death of Sir Charles. We knew him very well, for his favorite walk was over the moor to our house. He was deeply troubled by the curse which hung over the family, and when this tragedy came I naturally felt that there must be some grounds for the fears which he had expressed. I was naturally upset then when another member of the family came down to live here. I felt that he should be warned of the danger which he will meet. That was all that I meant to relate.

"But what is the danger?"

"You know the story of the hound?"

"I do not believe in such nonsense."

"But I do. If you have any influence with Sir Henry, take him away from a place which has always been fatal to his family. The world is wide. Why should he wish to live at the place of danger?"

"Because it *is* the place of danger. That is Sir Henry's nature. I fear that unless you can give me some more definite information than this it would be impossible to get him to move."

"I cannot say anything definite, for I do not know anything definite."

"I would ask you one more question, Miss

Stapleton. If you meant no more than this when you first spoke to me, why didn't you want your brother to overhear what you said? He shouldn't object to what you had to say."

"My brother is very anxious to have a Baskerville living in the Hall, because he thinks it would be good for the poor folk who live on the moor. He would be very angry if he knew that I have said anything which might encourage Sir Henry to go away. But I have done my duty now and I will say no more. I must go back, or he will miss me and suspect that I have seen you. Goodbye!" She turned and had disappeared in a few minutes among the scattered boulders, while I, with my soul full of shadowy fears, worked my way back to Baskerville Hall.

CHAPTER 8

First Report of Dr. Watson

From this point onward I will tell this story by drawing from my own letters to Mr. Sherlock Holmes which lie before me on the table. One page is missing, but otherwise they are exactly as written. They show my feelings and suspicions of the moment more accurately than my memory, clear as it is upon these tragic events, can possibly do.

Baskerville Hall, October 13th.

MY DEAR HOLMES:

My previous letters and telegrams have kept you pretty well up to date as to all that has occurred in this most God-forsaken corner of the world. The longer one stays here the more does the spirit of the moor sink into one's soul, its vastness, and also its grim charm. When you are in the middle of it, you have left all traces of modern England behind you. On the other hand, you are conscious everywhere of the homes and the work of the prehistoric people. On all sides of you as you walk are the houses of these forgotten folk, with their graves and the huge stone slabs which are said to have marked their temples. As you look at their gray stone huts against the scarred hillsides, you leave your own age behind. If you were to see a skin-clad, hairy man crawl out from the low door fitting a flint-tipped arrow on to the string of his bow, you would feel that his presence there was more natural than your own. The strange thing is that there were so many of them living on what must always have been most barren soil. I am no student of prehistory, but I could imagine that they were some unwarlike and tormented race who were forced to accept what no one else would occupy.

All this, however, has little to do with the mission you sent me on and will probably be very uninteresting to your extremely practical mind. I can still remember your complete lack of interest as to whether the sun moved around the earth or the earth around the sun. Let me, therefore, return to the facts concerning Sir Henry Baskerville.

If you have not had any report within the last few days it is because up to today there was nothing of importance to relate. Then something very surprising happened, which I shall soon tell you about. But, first of all, I must keep you in touch with some of the other factors in the present situation.

One of these, which I have hardly mentioned, is the escaped convict out on the moor. There is strong reason now to believe that he has gone far away. This likelihood is a great relief to the lonely inhabitants of this district. Two weeks have passed since his escape, during which he has not been seen and nothing has been heard of him. It is very hard to believe that he could have held out on the moor during all that time. Of course, any one of these stone huts would give him a hiding place. But there would be nothing for him to eat unless he were to catch and kill one of the moor sheep. We think, therefore, that he has gone, and the people sleep better as a result.

We are four able-bodied men in this household, so that we could take good care of ourselves. I confess, however, that I have had uneasy moments when I have thought of the Stapletons. They live miles from any help. There are one maid, an old manservant, the sister, and the brother, who is not a very strong man. They would be helpless in the hands of a desperate fellow like this Notting Hill criminal if he tried to break in to their house. Both Sir Henry and I were concerned about their situation. I suggested that Perkins the groom should go over to sleep there, but Stapleton refused to let him.

The fact is that our friend, the baronet, begins to display a considerable interest in our attractive neighbor. It is not surprising, for time hangs heavily in this lonely spot to an active man like him, and she is a very fascinating and beautiful woman. There is something tropical and foreign about her which forms a striking contrast to her cool and unemotional brother. Yet he also gives the idea of hidden fires. He certainly has a very strong influence over her, for I have seen her continually glance at him as she talked as if seeking approval for what she said. I trust that he is kind to her. There is a dry glitter in his eyes and a firm set of his thin lips, which goes with a positive and possibly a harsh nature. You would find him interesting. He came over to call upon Baskerville on that first day. The very next morning he took us both to show us the spot where the legend of the wicked Hugo is supposed to have begun. It was a trip of several miles across the moor to a place which is so dismal that it might have suggested the story. We found a short valley between rugged high rocks which led to an open, grassy space flecked over with white cotton grass. In the middle of it rose two great stones, worn and sharpened at the upper end until they looked like the huge rotting fangs of some monstrous beast. In every way it matched the scene of the old tragedy. Sir Henry was very interested and asked Stapleton more than once whether he did really believe that supernatural powers might interfere with the affairs of men. He spoke lightly, but it was clear that he was very serious.

Stapleton was cautious in his replies, but it was easy to see that he said less than he might. He seemed unwilling to express his whole opinion out of consideration for the feelings of the baronet. He told us of similar cases, where families had suffered from some evil influence, and he left us with the impression that he shared the popular view of the matter.

On our way back we stayed for lunch at Merripit House, and it was there that Sir Henry met Miss Stapleton. From the first moment that he saw her he appeared to be strongly attracted to her, and I am much mistaken if the feeling was not mutual. He referred to her again and again on our walk home, and since then hardly a day has passed that we have not seen something of the brother and sister. They will dine here tonight, and there is some talk of our going to visit them next week. One would imagine that such a match would be very welcome to Stapleton, and yet I have more than once noticed his disapproval when Sir Henry has been paying some attention to his sister. He is very attached to her, no doubt, and would lead a lonely life without her, but it would seem extremely selfish of him if he were to stand in the way of her making so brilliant a marriage. Yet I am certain that he does not wish their closeness to ripen into love, and I have noticed several times that he has tried to keep them apart. By the way, your instructions to me never to allow Sir Henry to go out alone will become very much more difficult if a love affair were to be added to our other difficulties. My popularity would soon suffer if I were to carry out your orders to the letter.

The other day—Thursday, to be more exact—Dr. Mortimer lunched with us. He has been digging up an ancient burial site at Long Down and has got a prehistoric skull which fills him with great joy. Never was there such a single-minded fanatic as he! The Stapletons came in afterward, and the good doctor took us all to the yew alley at Sir Henry's request to show us exactly how everything occurred upon that fatal night. It is a long, gloomy walk, the yew alley, between two high walls of clipped hedge, with a narrow band of grass upon either side. At the far end is an old tumble-down summer house. Halfway down is the moor gate, where the old gentleman left his cigar ash. It is a white wooden gate with a latch. Beyond it lies the wide moor. I remembered your theory and tried to picture all that had occurred. As the old man stood there he saw something coming across the moor, something which terrified him so that he lost his wits and ran and ran until he died of sheer horror and exhaustion. There was the long, gloomy tunnel down which he fled. And from what? A sheepdog of the moor? Or a ghostly hound, black, silent, and monstrous? Was there a human hand in the matter? Did the pale, watchful Barrymore know more than he cared to say? It was all dim and murky, but always there is the dark shadow of crime behind it.

One other neighbor I have met since I wrote last. This is Mr. Frankland, of Lafter Hall, who lives some four miles to the south of us. He is an elderly man, red-faced, white-haired, and loves a good fight. His passion is for the British law, and he has spent a large fortune in lawsuits. He fights for the mere pleasure of fighting and is equally ready to take up either side of a question, so that it is no wonder that he has found it a costly amusement. Sometimes he will block off a right-of-way and defy the parish to make him open it. At others he will with his own hands tear down some other man's gate and declare that a path has existed there from time immemorial, defying the owner to prosecute him for trespass. He knows a great deal about legal rights, and he applies his knowledge sometimes in favor of the villagers of Fernworthy and sometimes against them. He is at times either carried in triumph down the village street or else burned in effigy, according to his latest adventure. He is said to have about seven lawsuits on his hands at present, which will probably swallow up the remainder of his fortune and so take away his sting and leave him harmless for the future. Apart from the law, he seems a kindly, good-natured person, and I only mention him because you instructed me to send you some description of the people who surround us. He is also currently engaged in using his rather powerful telescope to look out over the moor all day in the hope of catching a glimpse of the escaped convict. If he would confine his energies to this all would be well, but there are rumors that he intends to prosecute Dr. Mortimer for grave-digging without the consent of the next of kin because he dug up the prehistoric skull in the burial pit on Long Down. He helps to keep our lives from being dull and gives a little comic relief where it is badly needed.

And now, having brought you up-to-date on the escaped convict, the Stapletons, Dr. Mortimer, and Frankland, of Lafter Hall, let me end on that which is most important. I will tell you more about the Barrymores, and especially about the surprising development of last night.

First of all, about the test telegram, which you sent from London in order to make sure that Barrymore was really here. I have already explained that the testimony of the postmaster shows that the test was worthless and that we have no proof one way or the other. I told Sir Henry how the matter stood, and he at once, in his straightforward manner, had Barrymore up and asked him whether he had received the telegram himself. Barrymore said that he had.

"Did the boy deliver it into your own

hands?" asked Sir Henry.

Barrymore looked surprised, and considered for a little time.

"No," said he, "I was in the storage room at the time, and my wife brought it up to me."

"Did you answer it yourself?"

"No; I told my wife what to answer and she went down to write it."

In the evening he returned to the subject on his own.

"I could not quite understand the reason for your questions this morning, Sir Henry," said he. "I trust that they do not mean that I have done anything to weaken your confidence?"

Sir Henry had to assure him that it was not so and made him feel better by giving him a large part of his old wardrobe. Now that Sir Henry's new London outfit has arrived, he doesn't need his old clothes.

Mrs. Barrymore interests to me. She is a heavy-set woman, very respectable, and tends to be strict and narrow-minded. You could hardly imagine a less emotional subject. Yet I have told you how, on the first night here, I heard her sobbing bitterly, and since then I have more than once noticed traces of tears upon her face. Some deep sorrow eats away at her heart. Sometimes I wonder if she has a guilty memory which haunts her, and sometimes I suspect Barrymore of being a bully. I have always felt that there was something odd about this man's character, but the adventure of last night brings all my suspicions to a head.

And yet it may seem a small matter in itself. You are aware that I am not a very sound sleeper, and since I have been on guard in this house my slumbers have been lighter than ever. Last night, about two in the morning, I was awakened by a stealthy step passing my room. I rose, opened my door, and peeped out. A long black shadow was trailing down the corridor. It was thrown by a man who walked softly down the passage with a candle held in his hand. He was in shirt and trousers, with no covering to his feet. I could only see his outline, but his height told me that it was Barrymore. He walked very slowly and cautiously, and there was something indescribably guilty and secretive in his whole appearance.

I have told you that the corridor is broken by the balcony which runs around the house, but that it continues along the farther side. I waited until he had passed out of sight and then I followed him. When I came around the balcony, he had reached the end of the farther hallway. I could see from the glimmer of light through an open door that he had entered one of the rooms. Now, all these rooms are unfurnished and unoccupied so that his expedition became more mysterious than ever. The light shone steadily as if he were standing motionless. I crept down the passage as noiselessly as I could and peeped around the corner of the door.

Barrymore was crouching at the window with the candle held against the glass. His profile was half turned toward me, and his face seemed to be tense with expectation as he stared out into the blackness of the moor. For some minutes he stood watching intently. Then he gave a deep groan and with an impatient gesture he put out the light. Instantly I made my way back to my room, and soon heard the secretive steps passing once more upon their return journey. Long afterward when I had fallen into a light sleep, I heard a key turn somewhere in a lock, but I could not tell where the sound came from. What it all means I cannot guess, but there is some secret business going on in this house of gloom which sooner or later we shall get to the bottom of. I do not trouble you with my theories, for you asked me to furnish you only with facts. I have had a long talk with Sir Henry this morning, and we have made a plan of action based upon my observations of last night. I will not speak about it just now, but it should make my next report interesting reading.

CHAPTER 9

Second Report of Dr. Watson: The Light Upon the Moor

Baskerville Hall, October 15th.

MY DEAR HOLMES:

If I failed to give you much news during the early days of my mission, you must agree that I am now making up for lost time. Events are crowding thick and fast upon us. In my last report I ended with Barrymore at the window, and now I have quite a summary of events which will, unless I am very mistaken, considerably surprise you. Things have taken a turn which I could not have foreseen. In some ways they have become much clearer and in some ways they have become more complicated. But I will tell you all and you shall judge for yourself.

Before breakfast on the morning following my adventure I went down the hallway and examined the room which Barrymore had entered the night before. The western window that he had stared through so intently has, I noticed, one characteristic above all other windows in the house—it commands the nearest view of the moor. There is an opening between two trees which enables one from this point of view to look right down upon it. All the other windows only give a person a distant glimpse of it. It follows, then, that Barrymore must have been looking out for something or somebody on the moor. The night was very dark, so that I can hardly imagine how he could have hoped to see anyone. I had thought, perhaps, that some romantic meeting was about to take place. That would have accounted for his stealthy movements and also for the uneasiness of his wife. The man is a good-looking fellow, very well-equipped to steal the heart of a country girl, so that this theory seemed reasonable. That opening of the door which I had heard after I had returned to my room might mean that he had gone out to keep some secret meeting. So I reasoned with myself in the morning, and I tell you the direction of my suspicions, even though the result may show that they were incorrect.

But whatever the true explanation of Barrymore's movements might be, I felt that the responsibility of keeping them to myself was more than I could bear. I had a talk with the baronet in his study after breakfast, and I told him all that I had seen. He was less surprised than

I had expected.

"I knew that Barrymore walked around at night, and I had a mind to speak to him about it," said he. "Two or three times I have heard his steps in the passage, coming and going, at just about the hour you name."

"Perhaps then he pays a visit every night to that particular window," I suggested.

"Perhaps he does. If so, we should be able to shadow him and see what it is that he is after. I wonder what your friend Holmes would do if he were here."

"I believe that he would do exactly what you now suggest," said I. "He would follow Barrymore and see what he did."

"Then we shall do it together."

"But surely he would hear us."

"The man is rather deaf, and in any case we must take our chance of that. We'll sit up in my room tonight and wait until he passes." Sir Henry rubbed his hands with pleasure. It was clear that he looked forward to the adventure as a relief from his overly quiet life upon the moor.

The baronet has been talking with the architect who prepared the plans for Sir Charles, and with a contractor from London, so that we may expect great changes to begin here soon. There have been decorators and furnishers up from Plymouth, and it is evident that our friend has large ideas and intends to spare no expense to restore the glory of his family. When the house is renovated and refurnished, all that he will need will be a wife to make it complete. Between us there are pretty clear signs who may fill this vacancy if the lady is willing, for I have rarely seen a man more love-struck over a woman than he is with our beautiful neighbor, Miss Stapleton. And yet the course of true love does not always run quite as smoothly as one would expect. Today, for example, its surface was broken by a very unexpected ripple, which has caused our friend considerable puzzlement and annoyance.

After the conversation which I have quoted about Barrymore, Sir Henry put on his hat and prepared to go out. As a matter of course I did the same.

"What, are you coming, Watson?" he asked, looking at me in an odd way.

"That depends on whether you are going out on the moor," said I.

"Yes, I am."

"Well, you know what my instructions are. I am sorry to intrude, but you heard how strongly Holmes insisted that I should not leave you, and especially that you should not go alone onto the moor."

Sir Henry put his hand upon my shoulder, with a pleasant smile.

"My dear fellow," said he, "Holmes, with all his wisdom, did not foresee some things which have happened since I have been living on the moor. You understand me? I am sure that you are the last man in the world who would wish to be a spoil-sport. I must go out alone."

It put me in a most awkward position. I was at a loss what to say or what to do, and before I had made up my mind he picked up his cane and was gone.

But when I began to think the matter over, my conscience condemned me bitterly for having allowed him to go out of my sight. I imagined what my feelings would be if I had to return to you and to confess that some misfortune had occurred due to my failure to follow your instructions. I assure you my cheeks flushed at the very thought. It might not even now be too late to overtake him, so I set off at once in the direction of Merripit House.

I hurried along the road as fast as I could without seeing anything of Sir Henry, until I came to the point where the moor path branches off. There, fearing that perhaps I had come in the wrong direction after all, I walked up a hill from which I could command a view—the same hill which is cut into the dark stone pit. From there I saw him at once. He was on the moor path about a quarter of a mile off, and a lady was by his side who could only be Miss Stapleton. It was clear that there was already an understanding between them and that they had planned to meet.

They were walking slowly along in deep conversation, and I saw her making quick little movements of her hands as if she were very sincere in what she was saying, while he listened intently, and once or twice shook his head in strong disagreement. I stood among the rocks watching them, very much puzzled as to what I should do next. I thought it would be outrageous to break up their intimate conversation, and yet my clear duty was never for an instant to let him out of my sight. To spy upon a friend was a hateful task. Still, I could see no better course than to watch him from the hill, and to clear my conscience by confessing to him afterward what I had done. It is true that if any sudden danger had threatened him I was too far away to be of use. Yet I am sure that you will agree with me that the situation was awkward, and that there was nothing more which I could do.

Our friend, Sir Henry, and the lady had halted on the path and were standing deeply absorbed in their conversation, when I was suddenly aware that I was not the only witness of their meeting. A wisp of green floating in the air caught my eye, and another glance showed me that it was carried on a stick by a man who was moving among the broken ground. It was Stapleton with his butterfly net. He was very much closer to the pair than I was, and he appeared to be moving in their direction. At this instant Sir Henry suddenly drew Miss Stapleton to his side. His arm was around her, but it seemed to me that she was straining away from him with her face turned. He stooped his head to hers, and she raised one hand as if in protest. Next moment I saw them spring apart and turn hurriedly around.

Stapleton was the cause of the interruption. He was running wildly toward them, his ridiculous net dangling behind him. His arms moved about and he almost danced with excitement in front of the lovers. What the scene meant I could not imagine, but it seemed to me that Stapleton was abusing Sir Henry, who offered explanations, which became angrier as the other refused to accept them. The lady stood by in proud silence. Finally Stapleton turned upon his heel and motioned in a firm way to his sister, who, after a doubtful glance at Sir Henry, walked off with her brother. The naturalist's angry gestures showed that the lady was included in his displeasure. The baronet stood for a minute looking after them, and then he walked slowly back the way that he had come. With his head hanging, he seemed the very picture of deep unhappiness.

What all this meant I could not imagine, but I was deeply ashamed to have witnessed so personal a scene without my friend's knowledge. I ran down the hill therefore and met the baronet at the bottom. His face was flushed with anger and his brows were wrinkled, like one who is at his wits ends what to do.

"Hello, Watson! Where have you dropped from?" said he. "You don't mean to say that you came after me in spite of all?"

I explained everything to him: how I had found it impossible to remain behind, how I had followed him, and how I had witnessed all that had occurred. For an instant his eyes blazed at me, but my honesty disarmed his anger, and he broke at last into a rather sad laugh.

"You would have thought the middle of that prairie a fairly safe place for a man to be private," said he, "but, by thunder, the whole countryside seems to have been out to see me do my wooing—and a mighty poor wooing at that! Where was your seat?"

"I was on that hill."

"Way in the back row, eh? But her brother was well up in front. Did you see him come out on us?"

"Yes, I did."

"Did he ever strike you as being crazy—this brother of hers?"

"I can't say that he ever did."

"I dare say not. I always thought him sane enough until today, but you can take it from me that either he or I ought to be in a straitjacket. What's the matter with me, anyhow? You've lived near me for some weeks, Watson. Tell me straight, now! Is there anything that would prevent me from making a good husband to a woman that I loved?"

"I should say not."

"He can't object to my worldly position, so it must be myself that he objects to. What does he have against me? I never hurt man or woman in my life that I know of. And yet he would not so much as let me touch the tips of her fingers."

"Did he say so?"

"That, and a good deal more. I tell you, Watson, I've only known her these few weeks, but from the first I just felt that she was made for me, and she, too—she was happy when she was with me, and that I'll swear. There's a light in a woman's eyes that speaks louder than words. But he has never let us get together and it was only today for the first time that I saw a chance of having a few words with her alone. She was glad to meet with me, but when she did it was not love that she would talk about, and she wouldn't have let me talk about it either if she could have stopped it. She kept coming back to it that this was a place of danger, and that she would never be happy until I had left it. I told her that since I had seen her I was in no hurry to leave it, and that if she really wanted me to go, the only way to work it was for her to arrange to go with me.

With that I offered in as many words to marry her, but before she could answer, down came this brother of hers, running at us with a face like a madman. He was just white with rage, and those light eyes of his were blazing with fury. What was I doing with the lady? How dared I offer her attentions which were distasteful to her? Did I think that because I was a baronet I could do what I liked? If he had not been her brother I should have known better how to answer him. As it was, I told him that I was not ashamed of my feelings toward his sister, and that I hoped that she might honor me by becoming my wife. That seemed to make the matter no better, so then I lost my temper too, and I answered him rather more hotly than I should perhaps, considering that she was standing by. So it ended by his going off with her, as you saw, and here am I as badly puzzled a man as any in this county. Just tell me what it all means, Watson, and I'll owe you more than I can ever hope to pay."

I tried one or two explanations, but, indeed, I was completely puzzled myself. Our friend's title, his fortune, his age, his character, and his appearance are all in his favor, and I know nothing against him unless it is this dark fate which runs in his family. The fact that his advances should be rejected so rudely without any reference to the lady's own wishes and that the lady should accept the situation without protest is very confusing. However, our guesses were put to rest by a visit from Stapleton himself that very afternoon. He had come to offer apologies for his rudeness of that morning. After a long private conversation with Sir Henry in his study, the result is that the conflict has been healed, and that we are to dine at Merripit House next Friday as a sign of it.

"I don't say now that he isn't a crazy man," said Sir Henry. "I can't forget the look in his eyes when he ran at me this morning, but I must admit that no man could make a better apology than he has done."

"Did he give any explanation of his conduct?"

"His sister is everything in his life, he says. That is natural enough, and I am glad that he should understand her value. They have always been together, and according to his account he has been a very lonely man with only her as a companion, so that the thought of losing her was really terrible to him. He had not understood, he said, that I was becoming attached to her, but when he saw with his own eyes that it was really so, and that she might be taken away from him, it gave him a tremendous shock.

For a moment he was not responsible for what he said or did. He was very sorry for all that had happened, and he recognized how foolish and how selfish it was that he should imagine that he could keep a beautiful woman like his sister to himself for her whole life. If she had to leave him, he would rather it be to a neighbor like myself than to anyone else. But in any case it was a blow to him and it would take him some time before he could prepare himself to meet it. He would withdraw all opposition if I would promise for three months to let the matter rest and to be content with the lady's friendship during that time without claiming her love. This I promised, and so the matter rests."

So there is one of our small mysteries cleared up. It is something to have touched bottom anywhere in this swamp in which we are floundering. We know now why Stapleton looked with disfavor upon his sister's suitor—even when that suitor was so eligible a one as Sir Henry. And now I pass on to another thread which I have picked out of the tangled coil. That is the mystery of the sobs in the night, of the tear-stained face of Mrs. Barrymore, of the secret journey of the butler to the western window. Congratulate me, my dear Holmes, and tell me that I have not disappointed you—that you do not regret the confidence which you showed in me when you sent me here. All these things have been thoroughly cleared up in one night.

I have said "in one night," but, in truth, it was by two nights' work, for on the first we came up empty. I sat up with Sir Henry in his rooms until nearly three o'clock in the morning, but we heard no sound except the chiming clock upon the stairs. It was a most depressing vigil and ended by each of us falling asleep in our chairs. Fortunately we were not discouraged, and we decided to try again. The next night we lowered the lamp and sat smoking cigarettes without making the least sound. It was incredible how slowly the hours crawled by! Yet we were helped through it by the same sort of patient interest which the hunter must feel as he watches the trap he has set to catch game. One struck, and two, and we had almost again given up in despair when, in an instant, we both sat bolt upright in our chairs with all our weary senses on high alert once more. We had heard the creak of a step in the passage.

Very quietly we heard it pass along until it died away in the distance. Then the baronet gently opened his door and we set out in pursuit. Our man had already gone around the gallery and the hallway was in complete darkness. Softly we stole along until we had come into the other wing. We were just in time to catch a glimpse of the tall, black-bearded figure, his shoulders rounded as he tiptoed down the passage. Then he passed through the same door as before, and the light of the candle framed it in the darkness and shot one single yellow beam across the gloom of the corridor. We shuffled cautiously toward it, trying every plank before we dared to put our whole weight upon it. We had taken the precaution of leaving our boots behind us, but, even so, the old boards snapped and creaked beneath our tread. Sometimes it seemed impossible that he could fail to hear our approach. However, the man is fortunately rather deaf, and he was entirely preoccupied in that which he was doing. When we finally reached the door and peeped through, we found him crouching at the window, candle in hand, his white, intent face pressed against the pane, exactly as I had seen him two nights before.

We had arranged no plan of attack, but the baronet is a man who likes to be direct. He walked into the room. As he did so, Barrymore sprang up from the window with a sharp hiss of his breath and stood, angry and trembling, before us. His dark eyes, glaring out of the white mask of his face, were full of horror and astonishment as he gazed from Sir Henry to me.

"What are you doing here, Barrymore?"

"Nothing, sir." His nervous excitement was so great that he could hardly speak, and the shadows sprang up and down from the shaking of his candle. "It was the window, sir. I go around at night to see that they are locked."

"On the second floor?"

"Yes, sir, all the windows."

"Look here, Barrymore," said Sir Henry sternly, "we have made up our minds to have the truth out of you, so it will save you trouble to tell it sooner rather than later. Come, now! No lies! What were you doing at that window?"

The fellow looked at us in a helpless way, and he wrung his hands together like one who is full of doubt and misery.

"I was doing no harm, sir. I was holding a candle to the window."

"And why were you holding a candle to the window?"

"Don't ask me, Sir Henry—don't ask me! I give you my word, sir, that it is not my secret, and that I cannot tell it. If it only concerned me, I would not try to keep it from you."

A sudden idea occurred to me, and I took the candle from the trembling hand of the butler.

"He must have been holding it as a signal," said I. "Let us see if there is any answer." I held it as he had done, and stared out into the darkness of the night. Uncertainly I could make out the black bank of the trees and the lighter expanse of the moor, for the moon was behind the clouds. And then I gave a cry of joy, for a tiny pinpoint of yellow light had suddenly broken through the dark veil, and glowed steadily in the center of the black square framed by the window.

"There it is!" I cried.

"No, no, sir, it is nothing—nothing at all!" the butler broke in; "I assure you, sir—"

"Move your light across the window, Watson!" cried the baronet. "See, the other moves also! Now, you rascal, do you deny that it is a signal? Come, speak up! Who is your partner-in-crime out there, and what is this secret plot that is going on?"

The man's face became openly defiant.

"It is my business, and not yours. I will not tell."

"Then you leave my employment right away."

"Very good, sir. If I must I must."

"And you go in disgrace. By thunder, you may well be ashamed of yourself. Your family has lived with mine for over a hundred years under this roof, and here I find you deep in some dark plot against me."

"No, no, sir; no, not against you!" It was a woman's voice, and Mrs. Barrymore, paler and more horror-struck than her husband, was standing at the door. Her bulky figure in a shawl and skirt might have been comic were it not for the intensity of feeling upon her face.

"We have to go, Eliza. This is the end of it. You can pack our things," said the butler.

"Oh, John, John, have I brought you to this? It is my doing, Sir Henry—all mine. He has done nothing except for my sake and because I asked him."

"Speak out, then! What does it mean?"

"My unhappy brother is starving on the moor. We cannot let him die at our gate. The light is a signal to him that food is ready for him, and his light out there is to show the spot to which to bring it."

"Then your brother is—"

"The escaped convict, sir—Selden, the criminal."

"That's the truth, sir," said Barrymore. "I said that it was not my secret and that I could not tell it to you. But now you have heard it, and you will see that if there was a plot it was not against you."

This, then, was the explanation of the secret expeditions at night and the light at the window. Sir Henry and I both stared at the woman in amazement. Was it possible that this modest, respectable person was of the same blood as one of the most notorious criminals in the country?

"Yes, sir, my name was Selden, and he is my younger brother. We spoiled him too much when he was a lad and let him have his own way in everything until he began to think that the world was made for his pleasure, and that he could do what he liked in it. Then as he grew older he met wicked companions, and the devil entered into him until he broke my mother's heart and dragged our name in the dirt. From crime to crime he sank lower and lower until it is only the mercy of God which has prevented him from being hanged. But to me, sir, he was always the little curly-headed boy that I had nursed and played with as an older sister would. That was why he broke out of prison, sir. He knew that I was here and that we could not refuse to help him. When he dragged himself here one night, weary and starving, with the guards hard at his heels, what could we do? We took him in and fed him and cared for him. Then you returned, sir, and my brother thought he would be safer on the moor than anywhere else until the excitement of his escape was over, so he hid there. But every second night we made sure if he was still there by putting a light in the window, and if there was an answer my husband took out some bread and meat to him. Every day we hoped that he was gone, but as long as he was there we could not desert him. That is the whole truth, as I am an honest Christian woman. So you see that if there is blame in the matter it does not lie with my husband but with me, for whose sake he has done all that he has."

The woman's words came with an intense sincerity which carried conviction with them.

"Is this true, Barrymore?"

"Yes, Sir Henry. Every word of it."

"Well, I cannot blame you for standing by your own wife. Forget what I have said. Go to your room, you two, and we shall talk further about this matter in the morning."

When they were gone we looked out of the window again. Sir Henry had flung it open, and the cold night wind beat in upon our faces. Far away in the black distance there still glowed that one tiny point of yellow light.

"I wonder how he dares," said Sir Henry.

"It may be so placed as to be only visible from here."

"Very likely. How far do you think it is?"

"Out by the Cleft Rock, I think."

"Not more than a mile or two off."

"Hardly that."

"Well, it cannot be far if Barrymore had to carry out the food to it. And he is waiting, this villain, beside that candle. By thunder, Watson, I am going out to capture that man!"

The same thought had crossed my own mind. It was not as if the Barrymores had taken us into their confidence. Their secret had been forced from them. The man was a danger to the community, a horrible scoundrel whom we could neither pity nor excuse. We were only doing our duty in taking this chance of putting him back where he could do no harm. With his brutal and violent nature, others would have to pay the price if we turned our backs. Any night, for example, our neighbors the Stapletons might be attacked by him, and it may have been the thought of this which made Sir Henry so eager to catch him.

"I will come," said I.

"Then get your revolver and put on your boots. The sooner we start the better, since the fellow may put out his light and leave."

In five minutes we were outside the door, starting upon our expedition. We hurried through the dark shrubbery, amid the dull moaning of the autumn wind and the rustle of the falling leaves. The night air was heavy with the smell of damp and decay. Now and again the moon peeped out for an instant, but clouds were driving over the face of the sky. Just as we came out on the moor a thin rain began to fall. The light still burned steadily in front.

"Are you armed?" I asked.

"I have a hunting whip."

"We must sneak up on him quickly, for he is said to be a desperate fellow. We shall take him by surprise and have him at our mercy before he can fight back."

"I say, Watson," said the baronet, "what would Holmes say to this? How about late at night when the power of evil is at its height?"

As if in answer to his words there rose suddenly out of the vast gloom of the moor that strange cry which I had already heard upon the borders of the great Grimpen Mire. It came with the wind through the silence of the night, a long, deep mutter then a rising howl, and then the sad moan in which it died away. Again and again it sounded, the whole air throbbing with it, shrill, wild, and menacing. The baronet caught my sleeve and his face glimmered white through the darkness.

"My God, what's that, Watson?"

"I don't know. It's a sound they have on the moor. I heard it once before."

It died away, and an absolute silence closed in upon us. We stood straining our ears, but nothing came.

"Watson," said the baronet, "it was the cry of a hound."

My blood ran cold in my veins, for there was a break in his voice which told of the sudden horror which had taken hold of him.

"What do they call this sound?" he asked.

"Who?"

"The country folk."

"Oh, they are ignorant people. Why should you mind what they call it?"

"Tell me, Watson. What do they say of it?"

I hesitated but could not escape the question.

"They say it is the cry of the Hound of the Baskervilles."

He groaned and was silent for a few moments.

"A hound it was," he said at last, "but it seemed to come from miles away, over there, I think."

"It was hard to say where it came from."

"It rose and fell with the wind. Isn't that the direction of the great Grimpen Mire?"

"Yes, it is."

"Well, it was up there. Come now, Watson,

didn't you think yourself that it was the cry of a hound? I am not a child. You need not fear to speak the truth."

"Stapleton was with me when I heard it last. He said that it might be the calling of a strange bird."

"No, no, it was a hound. My God, can there be some truth in all these stories? Is it possible that I am really in danger from so dark a cause? You don't believe it, do you, Watson?"

"No, no."

"And yet it was one thing to laugh about it in London, and it is another to stand out here in the darkness of the moor and to hear such a cry as that. And my uncle! There was the footprint of the hound beside him as he lay. It all fits together. I don't think that I am a coward, Watson, but that sound seemed to freeze my very blood. Feel my hand!"

It was as cold as a block of marble.

"You'll be all right tomorrow."

"I don't think I'll get that cry out of my head. What do you advise that we do now?"

"Shall we turn back?"

"No, by thunder; we have come out to get our man, and we will do it. We will go after the convict, and a hell-hound, as likely as not, will follow us. Come on! We'll see it through if all the devils of hell were loose upon the moor."

We stumbled slowly along in the darkness,

with the black outline of the rugged hills around us, and the yellow speck of light burning steadily in front. There is nothing so misleading as the distance of a light upon a pitch-dark night, and sometimes the glimmer seemed to be far away upon the horizon and sometimes it might have been within a few yards of us. But at last we could see from where it came, and then we knew that we were indeed very close. A flickering candle was stuck in a crack in the rocks which flanked it on each side in order to keep the wind from it and also to prevent it from being visible, except in the direction of Baskerville Hall. A granite boulder concealed our approach, and crouching behind it we gazed over it at the signal light. It was strange to see this single candle burning there in the middle of the moor, with no sign of life near it—just the one straight yellow flame and the gleam of the rock on each side of it.

"What shall we do now?" whispered Sir Henry.

"Wait here. He must be near his light. Let us see if we can get a glimpse of him."

The words were hardly out of my mouth when we both saw him. Over the rocks, in the crack where the candle burned, there was thrust out an evil yellow face, a terrible animal face, all seamed and scarred with evil emotions. Foul with mud, with a bristling beard, and hung with matted hair, it might well have belonged to one of those old savages who lived in the huts on the hillsides. The light beneath him was reflected in his small, sly eyes which peered fiercely through the darkness like a crafty and savage animal who has heard the steps of the hunters.

Something had evidently awakened his suspicions. It may have been that Barrymore had some private signal which we had neglected to give, or the fellow may have had some other reason for thinking that all was not well, but I could read his fears upon his wicked face. Any instant he might blow out the light and vanish in the darkness. Without hesitation, I sprang forward, and Sir Henry did the same. At the same moment the convict screamed out a curse at us and threw a rock which splintered up against the boulder which had sheltered us. I caught one glimpse of his short, squat, strongly built body as he sprang to his feet and turned to run. At the same moment by a lucky chance the moon broke through the clouds. We rushed over the top of the hill, and there was our man running with great speed down the other side, springing over the stones in his path with the energy of a mountain goat. A lucky shot from my revolver might have crippled him, but I had brought it only to defend myself if attacked and not to shoot an unarmed man who was running away.

We were both fast runners and in fairly good training, but we soon found that we had no chance of overtaking him. We saw him for a long time in the moonlight until he was only a small speck moving swiftly among the boulders upon the side of a distant hill. We ran and ran until we were completely out of breath, but the space between us grew ever wider. Finally we stopped and sat panting on two rocks, while we watched him disappearing in the distance.

And now a most strange and unexpected thing happened. We had risen from our rocks and were turning to go home, having given up the hopeless chase. The moon was low in the sky, and the jagged top of a granite tor stood up against the lower curve of its silver disc. There, outlined as black as an ebony statue on that shining background, I saw the figure of a man upon the tor. Do not think that it was a delusion, Holmes. I assure you that I have never in my life seen anything more clearly. As far as I could judge, the figure was that of a tall, thin man. He stood with his legs a little separated, his arms folded, his head bowed, as if he were brooding over that enormous wilderness of soil and granite which lay before him. He might have been the very spirit of that terrible place. It was not the convict. This man was far from the place where the latter had disappeared. Besides, he was a much taller man. With a cry of surprise I pointed him out to the baronet, but the second I grasped his arm the man was gone. There was the sharp summit of granite still cutting the lower edge of the moon, but its peak bore no trace of that silent and motionless figure.

I wished to go in that direction and to search the high rock, but it was some distance away. The baronet's nerves were still trembling from that cry, which recalled the dark story of his family, and he was not in the mood for fresh adventures. He had not seen this lonely man upon the tor and could not feel the thrill which his strange presence and his commanding attitude had given to me.

"A prison guard, no doubt," said he. "The moor has been thick with them since this fellow escaped." Well, perhaps his explanation may be the right one, but I would like to have some further proof of it. Today we mean to notify the Princetown people where they should look for their missing man. However, it's disappointing that we couldn't actually capture him ourselves. Such are the adventures of last night, and you must admit, my dear Holmes, that I have written you a very full report. Much of what I tell you is probably quite unimportant with regard to the case, but still I feel that it is best that I should give you all the facts and leave you to select those which will be most helpful to you in guiding you to your conclusions. We are certainly making some progress. So far as the Barrymores go, we have found the reason for their actions, and that has cleared up the situation very much. But the moor with its mysteries and its strange inhabitants remains as difficult to understand as ever. Perhaps in my next report I may be able to throw some light upon this also. It would be best if you could come out to us. In any case you will hear from me again in the course of the next few days.

CHAPTER 10

Extract from the Diary of Dr. Watson

So far I have been able to quote from the reports which I have forwarded during these early days to Sherlock Holmes. Now, however, I have arrived at a point in my narrative where I must abandon this method and trust once more to my memory, aided by the diary which I kept at the time. A few selections from the diary will carry me on to those scenes which are forever fixed in my mind. I continue then, from the morning which followed our unsuccessful chase of the convict and our other strange experiences out on the moor.

October 16th. A dull and foggy day with a drizzle of rain. The house is hemmed in with rolling clouds, which rise now and then to show the dreary curves of the moor, with thin, silver veins upon the sides of the hills, and the distant boulders gleaming where the light strikes upon their wet faces. It is depressing outside and in. The baronet is in a bad mood after the excitements of the night. I am conscious myself of a weight at my heart and a feeling of approaching danger—ever present danger, which is the more terrible because I am unable to define it.

And have I not cause for such a feeling? Consider the long chain of events which have all pointed to some evil influence which is at work around us. There is the death of the last occupant of the Hall, which exactly fulfilled the conditions of the family legend. Then there are the repeated reports from the common folk of the appearance of a strange creature upon the moor. Twice I have with my own ears heard the sound which resembled the distant baying of a hound. It is incredible, impossible, that it should really be outside the ordinary laws of nature. A ghostly hound which leaves material footmarks and fills the air with its howling is surely not to be thought of. Stapleton may go along with such a superstition, and Mortimer also, but if I have one quality upon earth it is common sense, and nothing will persuade me to believe in such a thing. To do so would be to descend to the level of these poor uneducated folk, who are not content with a mere demon dog but must insist on describing him with hell-fire shooting from his mouth and eyes. Holmes would not listen to such fantasies, and I am his aide. But facts are facts, and I have twice heard this crying out on the moor.

Suppose that there were really some huge hound loose upon it? That would go far to explain everything. But where could such a hound lie concealed, where did it get its food, where did it come from, how was it that no one saw it by day? It must be confessed that the natural explanation offers almost as many difficulties as the other. And always, apart from the hound, there is the fact of human involvement in London, the man in the cab, and the letter which warned Sir Henry against the moor. This at least was real, but it might have been the work of a protecting friend as easily as of an enemy. Where is that friend or enemy now? Has he remained in London, or has he followed us down here? Could he—could he be the stranger whom I saw upon the high rock?

It is true that I have had only the one glance at him, and yet there are some things to which I am ready to swear. He is no one whom I have seen down here, and I have now met all the neighbors. The figure was far taller than that of Stapleton, far thinner than that of Frankland. It might possibly have been Barrymore, but we had left him behind us, and I am certain that he could not have followed us. A stranger then is still dogging us, just as a stranger dogged us in London. We have never shaken him off. If I could lay my hands upon that man, then at last our difficulties might come to an end. To this one purpose I must now devote all my energies.

My first thought was to tell Sir Henry all my plans. My second and wisest one is to play my own game and speak as little as possible to anyone. He is silent and upset. His nerves have been strangely shaken by that sound upon the moor. I will say nothing to add to his fears, but I will take my own steps to reach my own goal.

We had a small scene this morning after breakfast. Barrymore asked permission to speak with Sir Henry, and they were together in his study for a little while. Sitting in the billiard room, I heard the sound of voices raised more than once, and I had a pretty good idea what was being discussed. After awhile, the baronet opened his door and called for me.

"Barrymore believes that he has a complaint," he said. "He thinks that it was unfair of us to hunt his brother-in-law down when he, of his own free will, had told us the secret."

The butler was standing very pale but very calm before us.

"I may have spoken too emotionally, sir," said he, "and if I have, I am sure that I beg your pardon. At the same time, I was very surprised when I heard you two gentlemen come back this morning and learned that you had been chasing Selden. The poor fellow has enough to fight against without my putting more upon his track."

"If you had told us of your own free will it would have been a different thing," said the baronet, "you only told us, or rather your wife only told us, when it was forced from you and you could not help yourself."

"I didn't think you would have taken advantage of it, Sir Henry—indeed I didn't."

"The man is a public danger. There are lonely houses scattered over the moor, and he is a fellow who will stop at nothing. You only need to get a glimpse of his face to see that. Look at Mr. Stapleton's house, for example, with no one but himself to defend it. There's no safety for anyone until he is under lock and key."

"He'll break into no house, sir. I give you my solemn word upon that. But he will never trouble anyone in this country again. I assure you, Sir Henry, that in a very few days the necessary arrangements will have been made and he will be on his way to South America. For God's sake, sir, I beg of you not to let the police know that he is still on the moor. They have given up the chase there, and he can lie quiet until the ship is ready for him. You can't tell on him without getting my wife and me into trouble. I beg you, sir, to say nothing to the police."

"What do you think, Watson?"

I shrugged my shoulders. "If he were safely out of the country it would relieve the taxpayer of a burden."

"But how about the chance of his attacking someone before he goes?"

"He would not do anything so insane, sir. We have provided him with all that he needs. To commit a crime would be to show where he was hiding."

"That is true," said Sir Henry. "Well, Barrymore—"

"God bless you, sir, and thank you from my heart! It would have killed my poor wife had he been caught again."

"I guess we are aiding and abetting a felony, Watson? But, after what we have heard I don't feel as if I could give the man up, so that's that. All right, Barrymore, you can go."

With a few broken words of gratitude the man turned, but he hesitated and then came back.

"You've been so kind to us, sir, that I should like to do the best I can for you in return. I know something, Sir Henry, and perhaps I should have said it before, but it was long after the inquest that I found it out. I've never breathed a word about it yet to mortal man. It's about poor Sir Charles's death."

The baronet and I were both upon our feet. "Do you know how he died?"

"No, sir, I don't know that."

"What then?"

"I know why he was at the gate at that hour. It was to meet a woman."

"To meet a woman! He?"

"Yes, sir."

"And the woman's name?"

"I can't give you the name, sir, but I can give you the initials. Her initials were L.L."

"How do you know this, Barrymore?"

"Well, Sir Henry, your uncle received a letter that morning. He usually got a great many letters, for he was a public man and well known for his kind heart, so that everyone who was in trouble was glad to turn to him. But that morning, as it happened, there was only this one letter, so I took more notice of it. It was from Coombe Tracey, and it was addressed in a woman's handwriting."

"Well?"

"Well, sir, I thought no more of the matter, and never would have had it not been for my wife. Only a few weeks ago she was cleaning out Sir Charles's study—it had never been touched since his death—and she found the ashes of a burned letter in the back of the grate. The greater part of it was charred to pieces, but one little slip, the end of a page, hung together, and the writing could still be read, though it was gray on a black background. It seemed to us to be a postscript at the end of the letter and it said: 'Please, please, since you are a gentleman, burn this letter, and be at the gate by ten o'clock.' Beneath it were signed the initials L.L."

"Have you got that slip?"

"No, sir, it crumbled all to bits after we moved it."

"Had Sir Charles received any other letters in the same writing?"

"Well, sir, I took no particular notice of his letters. I should not have noticed this one, only it happened to come alone."

"And you have no idea who L.L. is?"

"No, sir. No more than you have. But I expect if we could lay our hands upon that lady we should know more about Sir Charles's death."

"I cannot understand, Barrymore, why you came to hide this important information."

"Well, sir, it was immediately after that our own trouble came to us. And then again, sir, we were both of us very fond of Sir Charles, as we well might be considering all that he has done for us. To bring this up couldn't help our poor master, and it's best to go carefully when there's a lady in the case. Even the best of us—"

"You thought it might damage his reputation?"

"Well, sir, I thought no good could come of it. But now you have been kind to us, and I feel as if it would be treating you unfairly not to tell you all that I know about the matter."

"Very good, Barrymore; you can go." When the butler had left us Sir Henry turned to me.

"Well, Watson, what do you think of this new light?"

"It seems to leave the darkness rather blacker than before."

"So I think. But if we can only trace L.L. it should clear up the whole business. We have gained that much. We know that there is someone who has the facts if we can only find her. What do you think we should do?"

"Let Holmes know all about it at once. It will give him the clue which he has been looking for. I will be very much mistaken if it does not make him come out here."

I went at once to my room and drew up my report of the morning's conversation for Holmes. It was evident to me that he had been very busy lately, for the notes which I had received from Baker Street were few and short, and made no comment about the information which I had supplied. Also, they contained hardly any reference to my mission. No doubt his blackmailing case is demanding all his attention. And yet this new factor must surely capture his attention and renew his interest. I wish that he were here.

October 17th. All day today the rain poured down, rustling on the ivy and dripping from the eaves. I thought of the convict out upon the bleak, cold, shelterless moor. Poor devil!

Whatever his crimes, he has suffered much hardship to pay for them. And then I thought of that other one—the face in the cab, the figure against the moon. Was he also out in that storm—the unseen watcher, the man of darkness? In the evening I put on my raincoat and took a long walk out on the rain-soaked moor, full of dark imaginings, the rain beating on my face and the wind whistling around my ears. God help those who wander into the great mire now, for even the firm uplands are becoming a swamp. I found the black tor upon which I had seen the solitary watcher. From its jagged summit I looked out myself across the depressing fields. Gusts of rain drifted across their reddish-brown face, and the heavy, slate-colored clouds hung low over the landscape, trailing in gray wreaths down the sides of the fantastic hills. In the distant hollow on the left, half hidden by the mist, the two thin towers of Baskerville Hall rose above the trees. They were the only signs of human life which I could see, except for those prehistoric huts which lay crowded upon the slopes of the hills. Nowhere was there any trace of that lonely man whom I had seen on the same spot two nights before.

As I walked back, I was overtaken by Dr. Mortimer driving in his dog cart over a rough moorland track which led from the outlying farmhouse of Foulmire. He has been very attentive to us, and hardly a day has passed that he has not called at the Hall to see how we were getting on. He insisted upon my climbing into his dog cart, and he gave me a lift homeward. I found him to be very troubled over the disappearance of his little spaniel. It had wandered on to the moor and had never come back. I tried to console him as much as I could, but I thought of the pony on the Grimpen Mire, and I do not believe that he will see his little dog again.

"By the way, Mortimer," said I as we jolted along the rough road, "I suppose there are few people living around here that you do not know?"

"Hardly any, I think."

"Can you, then, tell me the name of any woman whose initials are L.L.?"

He thought for a few minutes.

"No," said he. "There are a few gypsies and working people whom I don't know, but among the farmers or upper-class people there is no one whose initials are those. Wait a bit though," he added after a pause. "There is Laura Lyons—her initials are L.L.—but she lives in Coombe Tracey."

"Who is she?" I asked.

"She is Frankland's daughter."

"What! Old Frankland the crank?"

"Exactly. She married an artist named Lyons, who liked to sketch out on the moor. He turned out to be a rascal and deserted her. But from what I hear, it may not have been all his fault.

Her father refused to have anything to do with her because she had married without his consent and perhaps for one or two other reasons as well. So, between the old sinner and the young one the girl has had a pretty bad time."

"How does she live?"

"I believe old Frankland gives her a small allowance, but it cannot be much, since most of his money is tied up in lawsuits. Whatever she may have deserved, people could not allow her to lose her good reputation altogether. Her story got out, and several of the people here did something to enable her to earn an honest living. Stapleton did, for one, and Sir Charles for another. I gave a small amount myself. It was to set her up in a typewriting business."

He wanted to know the reason for my questions, but I managed to satisfy his curiosity without telling him too much, for there is no reason why we should trust anyone. Tomorrow morning I shall go to Coombe Tracey, and if I can see this Mrs. Laura Lyons, a long step will have been made toward clearing up one link in this chain of mysteries. I am certainly developing the sneaky wisdom of the snake. When Mortimer kept pressing me with questions, I asked him casually what kind of skull Frankland had, and so heard nothing but craniology for the rest of our drive. I have not lived for years with Sherlock Holmes for nothing.

I have only one other incident to record upon this stormy and depressing day. This was my conversation with Barrymore just now, which gives me one more strong card which I can play in due time.

Mortimer had stayed for dinner, and he and the baronet played cards afterward. The butler brought me my coffee in the library, and I took the chance to ask him a few questions.

"Well," said I, "has this precious relation of yours departed, or is he still lurking out there?"

"I don't know, sir. I hope to heaven that he has gone, for he has brought nothing but trouble here! I have not heard from him since I left food for him the last time, and that was three days ago."

"Did you see him then?"

"No, sir, but the food was gone when I next went that way."

"Then he was certainly there?"

"So you would think, sir, unless it was the other man who took it."

I sat with my coffee cup halfway to my lips and stared at Barrymore.

"You know that there is another man then?"

"Yes, sir; there is another man upon the moor."

"Have you seen him?"

"No, sir."

"How do you know of him then?"

"Selden told me about him, sir, a week ago or more. He's in hiding, too, but he's not a convict as far as I can make out. I don't like it, Dr. Watson—I tell you straight, sir, that I don't like it." He spoke with passionate sincerity.

"Now, listen to me, Barrymore! I have no interest in this matter but that of your master. I have come here with no object except to help him. Tell me, honestly, what it is that you don't like."

Barrymore hesitated for a moment, as if he regretted his outburst or found it difficult to express his own feelings in words.

"It's all these goings-on, sir," he cried at last, waving his hand toward the rain-lashed window which faced the moor. "There's foul play somewhere, and there's black villainy brewing, to that I'll swear! Very glad I should be, sir, to see Sir Henry on his way back to London again!"

"But what is it that alarms you?"

"Look at Sir Charles's death! That was bad enough, for all that the coroner said. Look at the noises on the moor at night. There isn't a man would cross it after sundown if he was paid for it. Look at this stranger hiding out there, and watching and waiting! What's he waiting for? What does it mean? It means no good to anyone of the name of Baskerville, and I shall be very glad to be rid of it all on the day that Sir Henry's new servants are ready to take over the Hall."

"But about this stranger," said I. "Can you tell me anything about him? What did Selden say? Did he find out where he hid, or what he was doing?"

"He saw him once or twice, but he is a clever one and gives nothing away. At first he thought that he was the police, but soon he found that he had some hide-out of his own. A kind of gentleman he was, as far as he could see, but what he was doing he could not make out."

"And where did he say that he lived?"

"Among the old houses on the hillside—the stone huts where the old folk used to live."

"But how about his food?"

"Selden found out that he has got a lad who works for him and brings all he needs. I dare say he goes to Coombe Tracey for what he wants."

"Very good, Barrymore. We may talk further of this some other time." When the butler had gone, I walked over to the black window, and I looked through a blurred pane at the driving clouds and at the tossing outline of the wind-swept trees. It is a wild night indoors, and what must it be like in a stone hut upon the moor. What passion of hatred can it be which leads a man to hide in such a place at such a time! And what deep and important purpose can he have which calls for such a trial! There, in that hut upon the moor, seems to lie the very center of that problem which has disturbed me so much. I swear that another day shall not have passed before I have done all that a man can do to reach the heart of the mystery.

CHAPTER 11

The Man on the Tor

The excerpt from my private diary which forms the last chapter has brought my narrative up to the eighteenth of October, a time when these strange events began to move swiftly toward their terrible conclusion. The incidents of the next few days are forever marked upon my memory, and I can tell them without referring to the notes made at the time. I continue the story a day after I learned two important facts. One fact was that Mrs. Laura Lyons of Coombe Tracey had written to Sir Charles Baskerville and made an appointment with him at the very place and hour that he met his death. The other fact was that the other man hiding out on the moor could be found among the stone huts on the hillside. With these two facts in my possession, I felt that either my intelligence or my courage must be lacking if I could not shed some further light upon these dark places.

I had no opportunity to tell the baronet what I had learned about Mrs. Lyons the previous evening, for Dr. Mortimer played cards with him until it was very late. At breakfast, however, I informed him about my discovery and asked him whether he would care to accompany me to Coombe Tracey. At first he was very eager to come, but on second thought, it seemed to both of us that the results might be better if I went alone. The more formal we made the visit, the less we might learn. I left Sir Henry behind reluctantly, and drove off upon my new quest.

When I reached Coombe Tracey, I told Perkins to look after the horses, and I asked for the lady whom I had come to question. I had no difficulty in finding her rooms, which were central and nicely decorated. A maid showed me in without ceremony, and as I entered the sitting room a lady, who was sitting in front of a Remington typewriter, sprang up with a pleasant smile of welcome. Her face fell, however, when she saw that I was a stranger, and she sat down again and asked me the reason for my visit.

The first impression left by Mrs. Lyons was one of extreme beauty. Her eyes and hair were of the same rich hazel color, and her cheeks, though quite freckled, were flushed with an exquisite pink bloom. Admiration was, I repeat, the first impression. But the second was criticism. There was something slightly wrong with the face, some coarseness of expression, some hardness, perhaps, of eye, some looseness of lip which marred its perfect beauty. But these, of course, are afterthoughts. At the moment I was simply conscious that I was in the presence of a very fine-looking woman, and that she was asking me the reasons for my visit. I had not quite understood until that instant how delicate my mission was.

"I have the pleasure," said I, "of knowing your father." It was a clumsy introduction, and the lady made me feel it.

"There is nothing in common between my father and me," she said. "I owe him nothing, and his friends are not mine. If it were not for the late Sir Charles Baskerville and some other kind hearts I might have starved for all that my father cared."

"It was about the late Sir Charles Baskerville that I have come here to see you."

The freckles started out on the lady's face.

"What can I tell you about him?" she asked, and her fingers played nervously over the keys of her typewriter.

"You knew him, didn't you?"

"I have already said that I owe a great deal to his kindness. If I am able to support myself, it is largely due to the interest which he took in my unhappy situation."

"Did you exchange letters with him?"

The lady looked quickly up with an angry gleam in her hazel eyes.

"What is the object of these questions?" she asked sharply.

"The object is to avoid a public scandal. It is better that I should ask them here than that the matter should pass outside our control."

She was silent and her face was still very pale. At last she looked up with something reckless and defiant in her manner.

"Well, I'll answer," she said. "What are your questions?"

"Did you exchange letters with Sir Charles?"

"I certainly wrote to him once or twice to let him know that I appreciated his sensitivity and his generosity."

"Do you have the dates of those letters?"

"No."

"Have you ever met him?"

"Yes, once or twice, when he came into Coombe Tracey. He was a very shy and modest man, and he preferred to do good in secrecy."

"But if you saw him so seldom and wrote so seldom, how did he know enough about your affairs to be able to help you, as you say that he has done?"

She met my difficult question with complete readiness.

"There were several gentlemen who knew my sad history and united to help me. One was Mr. Stapleton, a neighbor and close friend of Sir Charles's. He was extremely kind, and it was through him that Sir Charles learned about my problems."

I knew already that Sir Charles Baskerville had allowed Stapleton to carry out charitable work for him on several occasions, so the lady's statement seemed truthful.

"Did you ever write to Sir Charles asking him to meet you?" I continued.

Mrs. Lyons flushed with anger again.

"Really, sir, this is a very remarkable question."

"I am sorry, madam, but I must repeat it."

"Then I answer, certainly not."

"Not on the very day of Sir Charles's death?"

The flush had faded in an instant, and a deathly face was before me. Her dry lips could not speak the "No" which I saw rather than heard.

"Surely your memory deceives you," said I. "I could even quote a passage of your letter. It ran 'Please, please, as you are a gentleman, burn this letter, and be at the gate by ten o'clock.'"

I thought that she had fainted, but she recovered herself by a supreme effort.

"Is there no such thing as a gentleman?" she gasped.

"You do Sir Charles an injustice. He did burn the letter. But sometimes a letter may be legible even when burned. You admit now that you wrote it?"

"Yes, I did write it," she cried, pouring out

her soul in a rush of words. "I did write it. Why should I deny it? I have no reason to be ashamed of it. I wished him to help me. I believed that if I had a talk with him, I could gain his help, so I asked him to meet me."

"But why at such an hour?"

"Because I had only just learned that he was going to London the next day and might be away for months. There were reasons why I could not get there earlier."

"But why a secret meeting in the garden instead of a visit to the house?"

"Do you think a woman could go alone at that hour to a bachelor's house?"

"Well, what happened when you did get there?"

"I never went."

"Mrs. Lyons!"

"No, I swear it to you on all I hold sacred. I never went. Something happened to prevent my going."

"What was that?"

"That is a private matter. I cannot tell it."

"You admit then that you made an appointment with Sir Charles at the very hour and place at which he met his death, but you deny that you kept the appointment."

"That is the truth."

Again and again I cross-questioned her, but I could never get past that point.

"Mrs. Lyons," said I as I rose from this long and inconclusive interview, "you are taking a very great responsibility and putting yourself in a very false position by not admitting all that you know. If I have to call in the aid of the police, you will find how seriously you are jeopardized. If your position is innocent, why did you at first deny having written to Sir Charles upon that date?"

"Because I feared that some false conclusion might be drawn from it and that I might find myself involved in a scandal."

"And why were you so insistent that Sir Charles should destroy your letter?"

"If you have read the letter you will know."

"I did not say that I had read the entire letter."

"You quoted some of it."

"I quoted the postscript. The letter had, as I said, been burned and was illegible. I ask you once again why it was that you were so insistent that Sir Charles should destroy this letter which he received on the day of his death."

"The matter is a very private one."

"The more reason why you should avoid a public investigation."

"I will tell you, then. If you have heard anything of my unhappy history you will know that I made a foolish marriage and had reason to regret it."

"I have heard so much."

"My life has been one unending storm of abuse from a husband whom I hate. The law is on his side, and every day I am faced by the possibility that he may force me to live with him. At the time that I wrote this letter to Sir Charles I had learned that there was hope of my regaining my freedom if certain expenses could be met. It meant everything to me—peace of mind, happiness, self-respect—everything. I knew Sir Charles's generosity, and I thought that if he heard the story from my own lips he would help me."

"Then how is it that you did not go?"

"Because I received help in the meantime from another source."

"Why then, did you not write to Sir Charles and explain this?"

"So I would have done had I not seen his death in the paper next morning."

The woman's story made a certain sense, and all my questions were unable to shake it. I could only check it by finding if she had, indeed, started divorce proceedings against her husband at or about the time of the tragedy.

It was unlikely that she would dare to say that she had not been to Baskerville Hall if she really had been, for a coach would be necessary to take her there, and could not have returned to Coombe Tracey until the early hours of the morning. Such a trip could not be kept secret.

The probability was, therefore, that she was telling the truth, or, at least, a part of the truth. I came away confused and disheartened. Once again I had reached that dead wall which seemed to block every path by which I tried to get at the object of my mission. And yet the more I thought of the lady's face and of her manner, the more I felt that she was hiding something. Why should she turn so pale? Why should she fight against every admission until it was forced from her? Why should she have been so quiet at the time of the tragedy? Surely the explanation of all this could not be as innocent as she would have me believe. For the time-being I could go no farther in that direction, but must turn back to that other clue which was hiding among the stone huts out on the moor.

And that was a most unclear direction. I realized it as I drove back and noted how hill after hill showed traces of the ancient people. Barrymore's only suggestion had been that the stranger lived in one of these abandoned huts, and many hundreds of them are scattered throughout the length and breadth of the moor. But I had my own experience for a guide since I had seen the man himself standing upon the summit of the Black Tor. That, then, would be the center of my search. From there I would explore every hut upon the moor until I lighted upon the right one. If this man were inside it, I would find out from his own lips, at the point of my revolver if necessary, who he was and why he had dogged us so long. He might slip away from us in the crowd of Regent Street, but it would be hard for him to do so out on the lonely moor. On the other hand, if I should find the hut and its tenant was not within it I must remain there, however long the wait, until he returned. Holmes had missed him in London. It would indeed be a triumph for me if I could track him down where my master had failed.

Luck had been against us again and again in this mystery, but now at last it came to my aid. And the messenger of good fortune was none other than Mr. Frankland, who was standing, gray-whiskered and red-faced, outside the gate of his garden, which opened on to the main road along which I traveled.

"Good-day, Dr. Watson," cried he with unusual good cheer, "you must really give your horses a rest and come in to have a glass of wine and to congratulate me."

My feelings toward him were very far from being friendly after what I had heard of his treatment of his daughter. On the other hand, I was anxious to send Perkins and the wagon home, and the opportunity was a good one. I got down from the wagon and sent a message to Sir Henry that I would walk over in time for dinner. Then I followed Frankland into his dining room.

"It is a great day for me, sir—one of the red-letter days of my life," he cried with many chuckles. "I have brought off a double event. I mean to teach them in these parts that law is law, and that there is a man here who does not fear to call upon it. I have established a right of way through the center of old Middleton's park, slap across it, sir, within a hundred yards of his own front door. What do you think of that? We'll teach these noblemen that they cannot ride roughshod over the rights of the commoners, curse them! And I've closed the wood where the Fernworthy folk used to picnic. These devilish people seem to think that there are no rights of property, and that they can swarm where they like with their papers and their bottles. Both cases have been decided, Dr. Watson, and both in my favor. I haven't had such a day since I had Sir John Morland convicted for trespassing because he shot in his own small game enclosure."

"How on earth did you do that?"

"Look it up in the books, sir. It will repay reading—Frankland v. Morland, Court of Queen's Bench. It cost me 200 pounds, but I got my verdict."

"Did it do you any good?"

"None, sir, none. I am proud to say that I had no interest in the matter. I act entirely from a sense of public duty. I have no doubt, for example, that the Fernworthy people will burn me in effigy tonight. I told the police last time they did it that they should stop these disgraceful demonstrations. The County police force is in a terrible state, sir, and it has not granted me the protection to which I am entitled. The case of Frankland v. Regina will bring the matter before the attention of the public. I told them that they would eventually regret their treatment of me, and already my words have come true."

"How so?" I asked.

The old man put on a very knowing expression.

"Because I could tell them what they are dying to know; but nothing would convince me to help the rascals in any way."

I had been trying to come up with an excuse so that I could get away from his gossip, but now I began to wish to hear more of it. I had seen enough of the pig-headed nature of the old sinner to understand that any strong sign of interest would be the surest way to stop him from revealing more information.

"Some poaching case, no doubt?" said I with an uninterested manner.

"Ha, ha, my boy, a very much more important matter than that! What about the convict on the moor?"

I stared. "You don't mean that you know where he is?" said I.

"I may not know exactly where he is, but I

am quite sure that I could help the police to lay their hands on him. Has it never struck you that the way to catch that man was to find out where he got his food and so trace it to him?"

He certainly seemed to be getting uncomfortably near the truth. "No doubt," said I; "but how do you know that he is anywhere upon the moor?"

"I know it because I have seen with my own eyes the messenger who takes him his food."

My heart sank for Barrymore. It was a serious thing to be in the power of this spiteful old busybody. But his next remark took a weight from my mind.

"You'll be surprised to hear that his food is taken to him by a child. I see him every day through my telescope upon the roof. He passes along the same path at the same hour, and to whom should he be going except to the convict?"

Here was luck indeed! And yet I suppressed all appearance of interest. A child! Barrymore had said that our unknown was supplied by a boy. It was on his track, and not upon the convict's, that Frankland had stumbled. If I could learn what he knew, it might save me a long and weary hunt. But disbelief and indifference were evidently my strongest cards.

"I should say that it was much more likely that it was the son of one of the moorland shepherds taking out his father's dinner."

The least appearance of opposition struck fire out of the old tyrant. His eyes gave me a poisonous look, and his gray whiskers bristled like those of an angry cat.

"Indeed, sir!" said he, pointing out over the wide-stretching moor. "Do you see that Black Tor over yonder? Well, do you see the low hill beyond with the thorn bush upon it? It is the stoniest part of the whole moor. Is that a place where a shepherd would be likely to set up his station? Your suggestion, sir, is a most absurd one."

I meekly answered that I had spoken without knowing all the facts. My meekness pleased him and led him to further revelations.

"You may be sure, sir, that I have very good grounds before I come to an opinion. I have seen the boy again and again with his bundle. Every day, and sometimes twice a day, I have been able—but wait a moment, Dr. Watson. Do my eyes deceive me, or is there at the present moment something moving upon that hillside?"

It was several miles off, but I could distinctly see a small dark dot against the dull green and gray.

"Come, sir, come!" cried Frankland, rushing upstairs. "You will see with your own eyes and judge for yourself."

The telescope, an impressive instrument mounted upon a tripod, stood upon the flat roof of the house. Frankland clapped his eye to it and gave a cry of satisfaction.

"Quick, Dr. Watson, quick, before he passes over the hill!"

There he was, sure enough, a small youngster with a little bundle upon his shoulder, working his way slowly up the hill. When he reached the crest I saw the ragged crude figure outlined for an instant against the cold blue sky. He looked around him with a sly and secretive air, as if he were one who dreads being hunted. Then he vanished over the hill.

"Well! Am I right?"

"Certainly, there is a boy who seems to have some secret errand."

"And what the errand is even a county policeman could guess. But not one word shall they have from me, and I bind you to secrecy also, Dr. Watson. Not a word! You understand!"

"Just as you wish."

"They have treated me shamefully—shamefully. When the facts come out in Frankland v. Regina, I bet that a thrill of indignation will run through the country. Nothing would convince me to help the police in any way. For all they cared it might have been me, instead of my effigy, which these rascals burned at the stake. Surely you are not going! You will help me to empty the wine bottle in honor of this great occasion!"

But I resisted all his invitations and succeeded in persuading him not to walk home with me. I kept to the road as long as his eye was on me, and then I struck off across the moor and made for the stony hill over which the boy had disappeared. Everything was working in my favor, and I swore that it should not be through lack of energy or effort that I would miss the chance which fortune had thrown in my way.

The sun was already sinking when I reached the top of the hill, and the long slopes beneath me were all golden-green on one side and gray shadow on the other. A haze lay low upon the farthest skyline, out of which jutted the fantastic shapes of Belliver and Vixen Tor. Over the wide expanse there was no sound and no movement. One great gray bird, a gull or curlew, soared aloft in the blue heaven. He and I seemed to be the only living things between the huge arch of the sky and the desert beneath it. The barren scene, the sense of loneliness, and the mystery and urgency of my task all struck a chill into my heart. The boy was nowhere to be seen. But down beneath me in a cleft of the hills there was a circle of the old stone huts, and in the middle of them there was one which had kept enough of a roof to act as a screen against the weather. My heart leaped within me as I saw it. This must be the burrow where the stranger hid. At last my foot was on the threshold of his hiding place—his secret was within my grasp.

As I approached the hut, I walked as carefully as Stapleton would do when with poised net he drew near the sitting butterfly. I satisfied myself that the place had indeed been used as a place to live. A crude pathway among the boulders led to the run-down opening which served as a door. All was silent within. The unknown might be hiding there, or he might be prowling on the moor. My nerves tingled with the sense of adventure. Throwing aside my cigarette, I closed my hand upon the butt of my revolver and, walking swiftly up to the door, I looked in. The place was empty.

But there were a number of signs that I had not tracked down a false scent. This was certainly where the man lived. Some blankets rolled in a raincoat lay upon that very stone slab upon which Stone Age man had once slept. The ashes of a fire were heaped in a crude grate. Beside it lay some cooking utensils and a bucket half-full of water. A litter of empty cans showed that the place had been occupied for some time. As I looked around, my eyes became accustomed to the dim light and I noticed a metal cup and a half-full bottle of liquor standing in the corner. In the middle of the hut a flat stone served the purpose of a table. Upon this stood a small cloth bundle—the same, no doubt, which I had seen through the telescope upon the shoulder of the boy. It contained a loaf of bread, canned meat, and two cans of peaches. As I set it down again after carefully looking at it, my heart leaped to see that beneath it there lay a sheet of paper with writing on it. I raised it, and this was what I read, roughly scrawled in pencil: "Dr. Watson has gone to Coombe Tracey."

For a minute I stood there with the paper in my hands thinking out the meaning of this brief message. It was I, then, and not Sir Henry, who was being dogged by this secret man. He had not followed me himself, but he had set a helper—the boy, perhaps—upon my track, and this was his report. Possibly he had noticed and reported every step I had taken out on the moor. Always there was this feeling of an unseen force, a fine net drawn around us with incredible skill and delicacy, holding us so lightly that it was only at some supreme moment that we realized that we were indeed entangled in its meshes.

If there was one report there might be others, so I looked around the hut in search of them. There was no trace, however, of anything of the kind. Nor could I discover any sign which might tell me more about the character or intentions of the man who lived in this unusual place, except that he must have a great deal of self-discipline and care little for the comforts of life. When I thought of the heavy rains and looked at the gaping roof I understood how firm his purpose must be to keep him in that inhospitable living space. Was he our deadly enemy, or was he our guardian angel? I swore that I would not leave the hut until I knew.

Outside the sun was sinking low and the west was blazing with scarlet and gold. Its reflection was shot back in ruddy patches by the distant pools which lay amid the great Grimpen Mire. There were the two towers of Baskerville Hall, and there a distant blur of smoke which marked the village of Grimpen. Between the two, behind the hill, was the house of the Stapletons. All was sweet and mellow and peaceful in the golden evening light, and yet as I looked at them my soul quivered at the uncertainty and the terror of that meeting which was soon to take place. With tingling nerves but a fixed purpose, I sat in the dark recess of the hut and waited with gloomy patience for its tenant to arrive. And then at last I heard him. Far away came the sharp clink of a boot striking upon a stone. Then another and yet another, coming nearer and nearer. I shrank back into the darkest corner and cocked the pistol in my pocket, determined not to reveal myself until I had an opportunity of seeing something of the stranger. There was a long pause which showed that he had stopped. Then once more the footsteps approached and a shadow fell across the opening of the hut.

"It is a lovely evening, my dear Watson," said a well-known voice. "I really think that you will be more comfortable outside than in."

CHAPTER 12

Death on the Moor

For a moment or two I sat breathless, hardly able to believe my ears. Then my senses and my voice came back to me, while a crushing weight of responsibility seemed in an instant to be lifted from my soul. That cold, intelligent, rather sarcastic voice could belong to only one man in the entire world.

"Holmes!" I cried—"Holmes!"

"Come out," said he, "and please be careful with the revolver."

I stooped as I came out the crude doorway, and there he sat upon a stone outside, his gray eyes dancing with amusement as they fell upon my astonished features. He was thin and worn, but clear and alert. His keen face had been bronzed by the sun and roughened by the wind. In his tweed suit and cloth cap he looked like any other tourist upon the moor. Somehow he had managed, with that catlike love of personal cleanliness which was one of his characteristics, to be as clean-shaven and as perfectly dressed as if he were in Baker Street.

"I never was gladder to see anyone in my life," said I as I shook his hand.

"Or more astonished, eh?"

"Well, I must confess to it."

"The surprise was not all on one side, I assure you. I had no idea that you had found my occasional retreat, still less that you were inside it, until I was within twenty paces of the door."

"My footprint, I presume?"

"No, Watson, I fear that I could not attempt to recognize your footprint amid all the footprints of the world. If you seriously desire to trick me, you must change the place where you buy your tobacco. For when I see the stub of a cigarette marked Bradley, Oxford Street, I know that my friend Watson is in the neighborhood. You will see it there beside the path. You threw it down, no doubt, when you boldly charged into the empty hut."

"Exactly."

"I thought as much—and knowing your admirable determination, I was convinced you were sitting in ambush, a weapon within reach, waiting for the tenant to return. So you actually thought that I was the criminal?"

"I did not know who you were, but I was determined to find out."

"Excellent, Watson! And how did you narrow your search? You saw me, perhaps, on the night of the convict hunt, when I was so lacking in caution as to allow the moon to rise behind me?"

"Yes, I saw you then."

"And have no doubt searched all the huts until you came to this one?"

"No, your boy had been observed, and that gave me a guide where to look."

"The old gentleman with the telescope, no doubt. I could not make it out when I first saw the light flashing upon the lens." He rose and peeped into the hut. "Ha, I see that Cartwright has brought up some supplies. What's this paper? So you have been to Coombe Tracey, have you?"

"Yes."

"To see Mrs. Laura Lyons?"

"Exactly."

"Well done! Our researches have evidently been running in the same direction, and when we combine our results I expect we shall have a fairly full knowledge of the case."

"Well, I am glad from my heart that you are here, for indeed the responsibility and the mystery were both becoming too much for my nerves. But how in the name of wonder did you come here, and what have you been doing? I thought that you were in Baker Street working out that case of blackmailing."

"That was what I wished you to think."

"Then you use me and still do not trust me!" I cried with some bitterness. "I think that I have deserved better at your hands, Holmes."

"My dear fellow, you have been invaluable to me in this as in many other cases, and I beg that you will forgive me if I have seemed to play a trick upon you. In truth, it was partly for your own sake that I did it, and it was my realization of the danger you were in which led me to come out and examine the matter for myself. Had I been with Sir Henry and you it is likely that my point-of-view would have been the same as yours, and my presence would have warned our very dangerous opponents to be on their guard. As it is, I have been able to get around as I couldn't possibly have done if I had been living in the Hall, and I remain an unknown factor in the business, ready to throw in all my weight at a crucial moment."

"But why keep me in the dark?"

"For you to know could not have helped us and might possibly have led to my discovery. You would have wished to tell me something, or in your kindness you would have brought me out some comfort or other, and so an unnecessary risk would be run. I brought Cartwright out with me—you remember the little chap at the express office—and he has seen after my simple wants: a loaf of bread and a clean collar. Why does man want more? He has given me an extra pair of eyes upon a very active pair of feet, and both have been invaluable."

"Then my reports have all been wasted!"— My voice trembled as I recalled the pains and the pride with which I had composed them.

Holmes took a bundle of papers from his pocket.

"Here are your reports, my dear fellow, and very well-thumbed, I assure you. I made excellent arrangements, and they have only been delayed one day before I received them. I must compliment you very much for the energy and the intelligence which you have shown over an extremely difficult case."

I was still rather annoyed over the deception which had been practiced upon me, but the warmth of Holmes's praise drove my anger from my mind. I felt also in my heart that he was right in what he said, and that it was really best for our purposes that I should not have known that he was out on the moor.

"That's better," said he, seeing the shadow rise from my face. "And now tell me the result of your visit to Mrs. Laura Lyons—it was not difficult for me to guess that you had gone to see her, for I am already aware that she is the one person in Coombe Tracey who might help us in the matter. In fact, if you had not gone today, it is extremely likely that I would have gone tomorrow."

The sun had set and dusk was settling over

the moor. The air had turned chilly and we withdrew into the hut for warmth. There sitting together in the twilight, I told Holmes of my conversation with the lady. He was so interested that I had to repeat some of it twice before he was satisfied.

"This is most important," said he when I had concluded. "It fills up a gap which I had been unable to bridge in this most complex affair. You are aware, perhaps, that a close relationship exists between this lady and the man Stapleton?"

"I did not know of a close relationship."

"There can be no doubt about the matter. They meet, they write, there is a complete understanding between them. Now, this puts a very powerful weapon into our hands. If I could only use it to detach his wife."

"His wife?"

"I am giving you some information now, in return for all that you have given me. The lady who is known here as Miss Stapleton is really his wife."

"Good heavens, Holmes! Are you sure of what you say? How could he have permitted Sir Henry to fall in love with her?"

"Sir Henry's falling in love could do no harm to anyone except Sir Henry. He took particular care that Sir Henry did not make love to her, as you have yourself observed. I repeat that the lady is his wife and not his sister."

"But why this complicated deception?"

"Because he foresaw that she would be much more useful to him if she appeared to be an unmarried woman."

All my unspoken instincts, my cloudy suspicions, suddenly took shape and centered upon the naturalist. In that indifferent colorless man, with his straw hat and his butterfly net, I seemed to see something terrible—a creature of unending patience and craft, with a smiling face and a murderous heart.

"It is he, then, who is our enemy—it is he who dogged us in London?"

"So I read the riddle."

"And the warning—it must have come from her!"

"Exactly."

The shape of some monstrous villainy, half seen, half guessed, loomed through the darkness which had surrounded me so long.

"But are you sure of this, Holmes? How do you know that the woman is his wife?"

"Because he has forgotten himself enough to tell you a true piece of his life story when he first met you, and I dare say he has regretted it ever since. He was once a schoolmaster in the north of England. Now, there is no one easier to trace than a schoolmaster. There are teacher's agencies which one may use to identify any man who has been in the profession. A little investigation showed me that a school had come to grief under horrible circumstances, and that the man who had owned it—the name was different—had disappeared with his wife. The descriptions agreed. When I learned that the missing man was devoted to the study of insects the identification was complete."

The darkness was rising, but much was still hidden by the shadows.

"If this woman is in truth his wife, where does Mrs. Laura Lyons come in?" I asked.

"That is one of the points where your research has shed light. Your interview with the lady has cleared the situation very much. I did not know about a projected divorce between herself and her husband. In that case, since she regarded Stapleton as an unmarried man, she probably counted on becoming his wife."

"And when she learns the truth?"

"Why, then we may find the lady of service. It must be our first duty to see her—both of us—tomorrow. Don't you think, Watson, that you have been away from your responsibility rather long? Your place should be at Baskerville Hall."

The last red streaks had faded away in the west and night had settled upon the moor. A few faint stars were gleaming in a violet sky.

"One last question, Holmes," I said as I rose. "Surely there is no need of secrecy between you and me. What is the meaning of it all? What is he after?"

Holmes's voice sank as he answered:

"It is murder, Watson—refined, cold-blooded, deliberate murder. Do not ask me for details. My nets are closing upon him, even as his are upon Sir Henry, and with your help he is already almost at my mercy. There is but one danger which can threaten us. It is that he might strike before we are ready to do so. Another day—two at the most—and I will have completed my case, but until then, guard Sir Henry as closely as a fond mother watching her sick child. Your mission today has justified itself, and yet I could almost wish that you had not left his side. Listen!"

A terrible scream—a long yell of horror and suffering burst out of the silence of the moor. That frightful cry turned the blood to ice in my veins.

"Oh, my God!" I gasped. "What is it? What does it mean?"

Holmes had sprung to his feet, and I saw his dark, athletic outline at the door of the hut, his shoulders stooping, his head thrust forward, his face peering into the darkness.

"Hush!" he whispered. "Hush!"

The cry had been loud on account of its intensity, but it had pealed out from somewhere far off on the shadowy plain. Now it burst upon our ears, nearer, louder, more urgent than before.

"Where is it?" Holmes whispered; and I knew from the excitement in his voice that he, the man of iron, was shaken to the soul. "Where is it, Watson?"

"There, I think." I pointed into the darkness.

"No, there!"

Again the agonized cry swept through the silent night, louder and much nearer than ever. And a new sound mingled with it, a deep, muttered rumble, musical and yet menacing, rising and falling like the low, constant murmur of the sea.

"The hound!" cried Holmes. "Come, Watson, come! Great heavens, if we are too late!"

He had started running swiftly over the moor, and I had followed at his heels. But now from somewhere among the broken ground immediately in front of us there came one last despairing yell, and then a dull, heavy thud. We halted and listened. Not another sound broke the heavy silence of the windless night.

I saw Holmes put his hand to his forehead like a man in panic. He stamped his feet upon the ground.

"He has beaten us, Watson. We are too late."

"No, no, surely not!"

"Fool that I was to not take action. And you, Watson, see what comes of abandoning your duty! But, by Heaven, if the worst has happened we'll avenge him!"

Blindly we ran through the gloom, blundering against boulders, forcing our way through gorse bushes, panting up hills and rushing down slopes, heading always in the direction from where those dreadful sounds had come. At every hill Holmes looked eagerly around him, but the shadows were thick upon the moor, and nothing moved upon its dreary face.

"Can you see anything?"

"Nothing."

"But, listen, what is that?"

We heard a low moan. There it was again upon our left! On that side a ridge of rocks ended in a sheer cliff which overlooked a stone-strewn slope. Some dark, irregular object was spread-eagled on its jagged face. As we ran toward it, the vague outline hardened into a definite shape. It was a man lying face-down on the ground, the head doubled under him at a horrible angle, the shoulders rounded and the body hunched together as if in the act of attempting a somersault. So distorted was his appearance that I could not for a moment realize that that moan had been the passing of his soul. Not a whisper, not a rustle, rose now from the dark figure over which we stooped. Holmes laid his hand upon him and held it up again with an exclamation of horror. The gleam of the match which he struck shone upon his blood-smeared fingers and upon the ghastly pool which widened slowly from the crushed skull of the victim. And it shone upon something else which turned our hearts sick and faint within us—the body of Sir Henry Baskerville!

There was no chance of either of us forgetting that odd reddish tweed suit—the very one which he had worn on the first morning that we had seen him in Baker Street. We caught the one clear glimpse of it, and then the match flickered and went out, even as the hope had gone out of our souls. Holmes groaned, and his face glimmered white through the darkness.

"The brute! the brute!" I cried with clenched hands. "Oh Holmes, I shall never forgive myself for having left him to his fate."

"I am more to blame than you, Watson. In order to have my case well-rounded and complete, I have thrown away the life of my client. It is the greatest blow which has befallen me in my career. But how could I know—how could I know—that he would risk his life alone upon the moor in the face of all my warnings?"

"That we should have heard his screams—my God, those screams!—and yet have been unable to save him! Where is this brute of a hound which drove him to his death? It may be lurking among these rocks at this instant. And Stapleton, where is he? He shall answer for this deed."

"He shall. I will see to that. Uncle and nephew have been murdered—the one frightened to death by the very sight of a beast which he thought to be supernatural, the other driven to his end in his wild flight to escape from it. But now we have to prove the connection between the man and the beast. Except from what we heard, we cannot even swear to the existence of the latter, since Sir Henry has evidently died from the fall. But, by heavens, clever as he is, the fellow shall be in my power before another day is past!"

We stood with bitter hearts on either side of the mangled body, overwhelmed by this sudden and unalterable disaster which had brought all our long and weary efforts to so pitiful an end. Then as the moon rose we climbed to the top of the rocks over which our poor friend had fallen. From the summit we gazed out over the shadowy moor, half silver and half gloom. Far away, miles off, in the direction of Grimpen, a single steady yellow light was shining. It could only come from the lonely home of the Stapletons. With a bitter curse I shook my fist at it as I gazed.

"Why should we not seize him at once?"

"Our case is not complete. The fellow is cautious and clever to the last degree. It is not what we know, but what we can prove. If we make one false move the villain may escape us yet."

"What can we do?"

"There will be plenty for us to do tomorrow. Tonight we can only perform the last services to our poor friend."

Together we made our way down the steep slope and approached the body, black and clear against the silvered stones. The agony of those twisted limbs struck me with a spasm of pain and blurred my eyes with tears.

"We must send for help, Holmes! We cannot carry him all the way to the Hall. Good heavens, are you mad?"

He had uttered a cry and bent over the body. Now he was dancing and laughing and shaking my hand. Could this be my stern, self-contained friend? These were hidden fires, indeed!

"A beard! A beard! The man has a beard!"

"A beard?"

"It is not the baronet—it is—why, it is my neighbor, the convict!"

With feverish haste we had turned the body over, and that dripping beard was pointing up to the cold, clear moon. There could be no doubt about the overhanging eyebrows, the sunken animal eyes. It was indeed the same face which had glared upon me in the light of the candle from over the rock—the face of Selden, the criminal.

Then in an instant it was all clear to me. I remembered how the baronet had told me that he had handed his old clothing to Barrymore. Barrymore had passed it on in order to help Selden in his escape. Boots, shirt, cap—it was all Sir Henry's. The tragedy was still black enough, but this man had at least deserved death by the laws of his country. I told Holmes how the matter stood, my heart bubbling over with thankfulness and joy.

"Then the clothes have been the poor devil's death," said he. "It is clear enough that the hound has been laid on from some article of Sir Henry's—the boot which was stolen in the hotel, in all probability—and so ran this man down. There is one very odd thing, however: How did Selden know, in the darkness, that the hound was on his trail?"

"He heard him."

"To hear a hound upon the moor would not work a hard man like this convict into such a frenzy of terror that he would risk recapture by screaming wildly for help. By his cries he must have run a long way after he knew the animal was on his track. How did he know?"

"A greater mystery to me is why this hound, assuming that all our guesses are correct—"

"I assume nothing."

"Well, then, why this hound should be loose tonight. I suppose that it does not always run loose upon the moor. Stapleton would not let it go unless he had reason to think that Sir Henry would be there."

"My difficulty is the more challenging of the two, for I think that we shall very shortly get an explanation of yours, while mine may remain a mystery forever. The question now is what shall we do with this poor wretch's body? We cannot leave it here to the foxes and the ravens."

"I suggest that we put it in one of the huts until we can contact the police."

"Exactly. I have no doubt that you and I could carry it that far. Hello, Watson, what's this? It's the man himself, by all that's wonderful and bold! Not a word to show your suspicions—not a word, or my plans crumble to the ground."

A figure was approaching us over the moor, and I saw the dull red glow of a cigar. The moon shone upon him, and I could distinguish the trim form and self-confident walk of the naturalist. He stopped when he saw us, and then came on again.

"Why, Dr. Watson, that's not you, is it? You are the last man that I would have expected to see out on the moor at this time of night. But, dear me, what's this? Somebody hurt? Not—don't tell me that it is our friend Sir Henry!" He hurried past me and stooped over the dead man. I heard a sharp intake of his breath and the cigar fell from his fingers.

"Who—who's this?" he stammered.

"It is Selden, the man who escaped from Princetown."

Stapleton turned his disgusting face to us. With a great effort he had overcome his amazement and his disappointment. He looked sharply from Holmes to me.

"Dear me! What a very shocking business! How did he die?"

"He appears to have broken his neck by falling over these rocks. My friend and I were strolling on the moor when we heard a cry."

"I heard a cry also. That was what brought me out. I was uneasy about Sir Henry."

"Why about Sir Henry in particular?" I could not help asking.

"Because I had suggested that he should come over. When he did not come I was surprised, and I naturally became alarmed for his safety when I heard cries upon the moor. By the way"—his eyes darted again from my face to Holmes's—"did you hear anything else besides a cry?"

"No," said Holmes; "did you?"

"No."

"What do you mean, then?"

"Oh, you know the stories that the local folk tell about a phantom hound, and so on. It is said to be heard at night upon the moor. I was wondering if anyone heard such a sound tonight."

"We heard nothing of the kind," said I.

"And what is your theory of this poor fellow's death?"

"I have no doubt that fear and a lack of food and shelter drove him out of his mind. He has rushed about the moor in a crazy state and eventually fallen over here and broken his neck."

"That seems the most reasonable theory," said Stapleton, and he gave what appeared to be a sigh of relief. "What do you think about it, Mr. Sherlock Holmes?"

My friend bowed his greeting.

"You are quick at identification," said he.

"We have been expecting you in these parts since Dr. Watson came here. You are in time to see a tragedy."

"Yes, indeed. I have no doubt that my friend's explanation will cover the facts. I will take an unpleasant memory back to London with me tomorrow."

"Oh, you return tomorrow?"

"That is my plan."

"I hope your visit has cast some light upon those events which have puzzled us?"

Holmes shrugged his shoulders.

"One cannot always be successful. An investigator needs facts and not legends or rumors. It has not been a satisfactory case."

My friend spoke in his most direct and unconcerned manner. Stapleton still looked hard at him. Then he turned to me.

"I would suggest carrying this poor fellow to my house, but it would give my sister such a fright that I don't feel right in doing it. I think that if we put something over his face he will be safe until morning."

And so it was arranged. Resisting Stapleton's

offer of hospitality, Holmes and I set off to Baskerville Hall, leaving the naturalist to return alone. Looking back, we saw his figure moving slowly away over the broad moor, and behind him that one black smudge on the silvered slope which showed where Selden had come to his horrible end.

"We're getting a tight hold at last," said Holmes as we walked together across the moor. "What nerve the fellow has! How he pulled himself together in the face of what must have been a paralyzing shock when he found that the wrong man had fallen a victim to his plot. I told you in London, Watson, and I tell you now again that we have never had an enemy more worthy of our steel."

"I am sorry that he has seen you."

"And so was I at first. But there was no getting out of it."

"What effect do you think it will have upon his plans now that he knows you are here?"

"It may cause him to be more cautious, or it may drive him to desperate measures at once. Like most clever criminals, he may be over-confident and imagine that he has completely deceived us."

"Why shouldn't we arrest him at once?"

"My dear Watson, you were born to be a man of action. Your instinct is always to do something energetic. But supposing, for argument's sake, that we had him arrested tonight, what on earth the better off should we be for that? We can't prove anything against him. There's the devilish cleverness of it! If he were acting through a human accomplice we could get some evidence, but if we were to drag this great dog to the light of day it would not help us in putting a rope around the neck of its master."

"Surely we have a case."

"Not a shadow of one—only guesses and theories. We would be laughed out of court if we came with such a story and such evidence."

"There is Sir Charles's death."

"Found dead without a mark upon him. You and I know that he died of sheer fright, and we know also what frightened him but how are we to get twelve unexcitable jurymen to know it? What signs are there of a hound? Where are the marks of its fangs? Of course we know that a hound does not bite a dead body and that Sir Charles was dead even before the brute overtook him. But we have to prove all this, and we are not in a position to do it."

"Well, then, tonight?"

"We are not much better off tonight. Again, there was no direct connection between the hound and the man's death. We never saw the hound. We heard it, but we could not prove that it was running after this man's trail. There is a complete absence of motive. No, my dear fellow; we must accept the fact that we have no case at present, and that we need to run any risk in order to establish one."

"And how do you propose to do so?"

"I have great hopes of what Mrs. Laura Lyons may do for us when the situation is made clear to her. And I have my own plan as well. There is a tremendous amount of evil involved; but I hope before the day is over to have the upper hand at last."

I could draw nothing further from him, and he walked, lost in thought, as far as the Baskerville gates.

"Are you coming up?"

"Yes, I see no reason to hide any longer. But one last word, Watson. Say nothing of the hound to Sir Henry. Let him think that Selden's death was as Stapleton wants us to believe. He will have more courage for the ordeal which he will have to face tomorrow, when he is scheduled, if I remember your report correctly, to dine with these people."

"And so am I."

"Then you must excuse yourself and he must go alone. That will be easily arranged. And now, even though we are too late for lunch, I think that we are both ready for our dinners."

CHAPTER 13

Fixing the Nets

Sir Henry was more pleased than surprised to see Sherlock Holmes. He had started to expect that recent events would bring him out from London. He did raise his eyebrows, however, when he found that my friend had neither any luggage nor any explanations for its absence. Between us we soon supplied his wants. Then over a belated dinner we explained to the baronet as much of our experience as we wanted him to know. But first I had the unpleasant duty of breaking the news to Barrymore and his wife. To him it may have been a great relief, but she wept bitterly in her apron. To the entire world he was a man of violence, half animal and half demon; but to her he always remained the little willful boy of her own girlhood, the child who had clung to her hand. Evil indeed is the man who has not one woman to mourn him.

"I've been moping in the house all day since Watson went off in the morning," said the baronet. "I guess I should get some credit, for I have kept my promise. If I hadn't sworn not to go out alone I might have had a more lively evening, for I had a message from Stapleton asking me over there."

"I have no doubt that you would have had a more lively evening," said Holmes dryly. "By the way, I don't suppose you appreciate that we have been mourning over you for having broken your neck?"

Sir Henry opened his eyes. "How was that?"

"This poor wretch was dressed in your clothes. I fear your servant who gave them to him may get into trouble with the police."

"That is unlikely. There was no mark on any of them, as far as I know."

"That's lucky for him—in fact, it's lucky for all of you, since you are all on the wrong side of the law in this matter. I am not sure that as an honest detective my first duty is not to arrest the whole household. Watson's reports are most incriminating documents."

"But how about the case?" asked the baronet. "Have you made anything out of the tangle? I don't know that Watson and I are much the wiser since we came out here."

"I think that I shall be in a position to clear up the situation before long. It has been an extremely difficult and most complicated business. There are several points which are still cloudy—but it is coming all the same."

"We've had one experience, as Watson has no doubt told you. We heard the hound on the moor, so I can swear that it is not all empty superstition. I had something to do with dogs when I was out West, and I know one when I hear one. If you can muzzle that one and put him on a chain, I'll be ready to swear you are the greatest detective of all time."

"I think I will be able to muzzle him and chain him if you will give me your help."

"Whatever you tell me to do I will do."

"Very good; and I will ask you also to do it blindly, without always asking the reason."

"Just as you like."

"If you will do this, I think the chances are that our little problem will soon be solved. I have no doubt"

He stopped suddenly and stared fixedly up over my head into the air. The lamp beat upon his face, and so intent was it and so still that it might have been that of a clear-cut classical statue, a personification of alertness and expectation.

"What is it?" we both cried.

I could see as he looked down that he was hiding some emotion. His features were still composed, but his eyes shone with amused triumph.

"Excuse the admiration of an art expert," said he as he waved his hand toward the line of portraits which covered the opposite wall. "Watson won't admit that I know anything about art, but that is pure jealousy because we have different tastes. Now, these are a really very fine series of portraits."

"Well, I'm glad to hear you say so," said Sir Henry, glancing with some surprise at my friend. "I don't pretend to know much about these things, and I'd be a better judge of a horse or a steer than of a picture. I didn't know that you found time for such things."

"I know what is good when I see it, and I see it now. That's a Kneller, I'll swear, that lady in the blue silk over yonder, and the stout gentleman with the wig appears to be a Reynolds. They are all family portraits, I imagine?"

"Every one."

"Do you know the names?"

"Barrymore has been coaching me in them, and I think I can say my lessons fairly well."

"Who is the gentleman with the telescope?"

"That is Rear-Admiral Baskerville, who served under Rodney in the West Indies. The man with the blue coat and the roll of paper is Sir William Baskerville, who was an important figure in government when Pitt was Prime Minister."

"And this gentleman opposite to me—the one with the black velvet and the lace?"

"Ah, you have a right to know about him. That is the cause of all the mischief, the wicked

Hugo, who started the Hound of the Baskervilles. We're not likely to forget him."

I gazed with interest and some surprise upon the portrait.

"Dear me!" said Holmes, "he seems like a quiet, meek-mannered man, but I dare say that there was a devil hidden in his eyes. I had pictured him as a more powerful and bullying person."

"There's no doubt that the portrait is genuine, for the name and the date, 1647, are on the back of the canvas."

Holmes said little more, but the picture of the old ruffian seemed to fascinate him, and his eyes were continually fixed upon it during supper. It was not until later, when Sir Henry had gone to his room, that I was able to follow the direction of his thoughts. He led me back into the banqueting hall, his bedroom candle in his hand, and he held it up against the time-stained portrait on the wall.

"Do you see anything there?"

I looked at the broad plumed hat, the curling love-locks, the white lace collar, and the straight, severe face which was framed between them. It was not a brutal face, but it was hard and stern, with a firm-set, thin-lipped mouth, and a coldly critical eye.

"Is it like anyone you know?"

"There is something of Sir Henry about the

jaw."

"Just a suggestion, perhaps. But wait an instant!" He stood upon a chair, and, holding up the light in his left hand, he curved his right arm over the broad hat and round the long ringlets.

"Good heavens!" I cried in amazement.

The face of Stapleton had sprung out of the canvas.

"Ha, you see it now. My eyes have been trained to examine faces and not their trimmings. It is the first requirement of a criminal investigator that he should be able to see through a disguise."

"But this is marvelous. It might be his portrait."

"Yes, it is an interesting instance of a throwback, which appears to be both physical and spiritual. A study of family portraits is enough to convert a man to the idea that humans can be reborn in another lifetime. The fellow is a Baskerville—that is clear."

"With plans to gain the family fortune."

"Exactly. This chance viewing of the picture has supplied us with one of our most obvious missing links. We have him, Watson, we have him, and I dare swear that before tomorrow night he will be fluttering in our net as helpless as one of his own butterflies. A mounting pin, a cork, and a card, and we add him to the Baker Street collection!" He burst into one of his rare fits of laughter as he turned away from the picture. I have not heard him laugh often, and it has always foretold bad news for somebody.

I was up early in the morning, but Holmes was walking around even earlier, for I saw him as I dressed, coming up the drive.

"Yes, we should have a full day today," he remarked, and he rubbed his hands with the joy of action. "The nets are all in place, and the fishing is about to begin. We'll know before the day is over whether we have caught our big fish, or whether he has gotten through the nets."

"Have you been on the moor already?"

"I have sent a report from Grimpen to Princetown telling them of the death of Selden. I think I can promise that they will not bother you about it. And I have also notified my faithful Cartwright, who would have pined away at the door of my hut, as a dog does at his master's grave, if I had not set his mind at rest about my safety."

"What is the next move?"

"To see Sir Henry. Ah, here he is!"

"Good morning, Holmes," said the baronet. "You look like a general who is planning a battle with his chief-of-staff."

"That is the exact situation. Watson was asking for orders."

"And so do I."

"Very good. You are expected, as I understand, to dine with our friends the Stapletons tonight."

"I hope that you will come also. They are very hospitable people, and I am sure that they would be very glad to see you."

"I fear that Watson and I must go to London."

"To London?"

"Yes, I think that we should be more useful there at the present time."

The baronet's face fell.

"I hoped that you were going to see me through this business. The Hall and the moor are not very pleasant places when one is alone."

"My dear fellow, you must trust me unquestioningly and do exactly what I tell you. You can tell your friends that we would have been happy to have come with you, but that important business required us to be in town. We hope very soon to return to Devonshire. Will you remember to give them that message?"

"If you insist upon it."

"There is no other choice, I assure you."

I saw by the baronet's clouded brow that he was deeply hurt by what he regarded as our desertion.

"When do you wish to go?" he asked coldly.

"Immediately after breakfast. We will drive in to Coombe Tracey, but Watson will leave his things as a pledge that he will come back to you.

Watson, you will send a note to Stapleton to tell him that you regret that you cannot come."

"I have a good mind to go to London with you," said the baronet. "Why should I stay here alone?"

"Because it is your post of duty. Because you gave me your word that you would do as you were told, and I tell you to stay."

"All right, then, I'll stay."

"One more direction! I wish you to drive to Merripit House. Send back your carriage, however, and let them know that you intend to walk home."

"To walk across the moor?"

"Yes."

"But that is the very thing which you have so often cautioned me not to do."

"This time you may do it with safety. If I didn't have every confidence in your nerve and courage I would not suggest it, but it is absolutely necessary that you should do it."

"Then I will do it."

"And as you value your life, do not go across the moor in any direction except along the straight path which leads from Merripit House to the Grimpen Road, and is your natural way home."

"I will do just what you say."

"Very good. I would be glad to get away as soon after breakfast as possible, so as to reach

London in the afternoon."

I was astounded by this plan, although I remembered that Holmes had said to Stapleton the night before that his visit would end next day. It had not crossed my mind however, that he would wish me to go with him. I also could not understand how we could both be absent at a moment which he himself declared to be so important. There was nothing to do, however, but obey his orders; so we bade goodbye to our sad friend. A couple of hours afterward we were at the station of Coombe Tracey and had sent the carriage back on its return journey. A small boy was waiting on the platform.

"Any orders, sir?"

"You will take this train to town, Cartwright. The moment you arrive you will send a telegram to Sir Henry Baskerville, in my name, to say that if he finds the billfold which I have dropped, he is to send it by registered mail to Baker Street."

"Yes, sir."

"And ask at the station office if there is a message for me."

The boy returned with a telegram, which Holmes handed to me. It read:

Telegram received. Coming down with unsigned warrant. Arrive five-forty.

Lestrade.

"That is in answer to mine of this morning.

He is the best of the professional detectives, I think, and we may need his help. Now, Watson, I think that we cannot use our time better than by calling upon your acquaintance, Mrs. Laura Lyons."

His plan of attack was becoming clear. He would use the baronet in order to convince the Stapletons that we were really gone, while we would actually return at the instant when we were likely to be needed. That telegram from London, if mentioned by Sir Henry to the Stapletons, must remove the last suspicions from their minds. Already I seemed to see our nets drawing closer around that big fish.

Mrs. Laura Lyons was in her office, and Sherlock Holmes opened his interview with an honesty and directness which considerably amazed her.

"I am investigating the circumstances which surrounded the death of the late Sir Charles Baskerville," said he. "My friend here, Dr. Watson, has informed me of what you have said, and also of what you have failed to say in connection with that matter."

"What have I failed to say?" she asked defiantly.

"You have confessed that you asked Sir Charles to be at the gate at ten o'clock. We know that that was the place and hour of his death. You have failed to tell what the connection is between these events."

"There is no connection."

"In that case the coincidence is an amazing one. But I think that we shall succeed in establishing a connection, after all. I wish to be perfectly honest with you, Mrs. Lyons. We regard this case as one of murder, and the evidence may involve not only your friend Mr. Stapleton but his wife as well."

The lady sprang from her chair.

"His wife!" she cried.

"The fact is no longer a secret. The person who has passed for his sister is really his wife."

Mrs. Lyons sat down again. Her hands were grasping the arms of her chair, and I saw that the pink nails had turned white with the pressure of her grip.

"His wife!" she said again. "His wife! He is not a married man."

Sherlock Holmes shrugged his shoulders.

"Prove it to me! Prove it to me! And if you can do so—!" The fierce flash of her eyes said more than any words.

"I have come prepared to do so," said Holmes, drawing several papers from his pocket. "Here is a photograph of the couple taken in York four years ago. It is inscribed 'Mr. and Mrs. Vandeleur,' but it will not be difficult for you to recognize him, and her also, if you know her by sight. Here are three written descriptions by trustworthy witnesses of Mr. and Mrs. Vandeleur, who at that time ran St. Oliver's private school. Read them and see if you can doubt the identity of these people."

She glanced at them, and then looked up at us with the stony face of a desperate woman.

"Mr. Holmes," she said, "this man had offered me marriage on condition that I could get a divorce from my husband. He has lied to me, the villain, in every imaginable way. Not one word of truth has he ever told me. And why—why? I imagined that all was for my own sake. But now I see that I was never anything but a tool in his hands. Why should I keep faith with him who never kept any with me? Why should I try to shield him from the consequences of his own wicked acts? Ask me what you like, and there is nothing which I shall hold back. One thing I swear to you, and that is that when I wrote the letter I never dreamed of any harm to the old gentleman, who had been my kindest friend."

"I entirely believe you, madam," said Sherlock Holmes.

"Discussing these events must be very painful to you, and perhaps it will make it easier if I tell you what occurred, and you can check me if I make any factual mistake. The sending of this letter was suggested to you by Stapleton?"

"He dictated it."

"I believe that the reason he gave was that

you would receive help from Sir Charles for the legal expenses connected with your divorce?"

"Exactly."

"And then after you had sent the letter he discouraged you from keeping the appointment?"

"He told me that it would hurt his self-respect if any other man should give me money to obtain a divorce, and that though he was a poor man himself he would spend his last penny to remove the obstacles which divided us."

"He appears to have a very unchanging character. And then you heard nothing until you read the reports of the death in the paper?"

"No."

"And he made you swear to say nothing about your appointment with Sir Charles?"

"He did. He said that the death was a very mysterious one, and that I should certainly be suspected if the facts came out. He frightened me into remaining silent."

"Quite so. But you had your suspicions?"

She hesitated and looked down.

"I knew him," she said. "But if he had been honest with me I would always have been loyal to him."

"I think that on the whole you have had a fortunate escape," said Sherlock Holmes. "You have had him in your power and he knew it, and yet you are alive. You have been walking for some months very near to the edge of a cliff. We must wish you good morning now, Mrs. Lyons, and it is likely that you will soon hear from us again."

"Our case becomes rounded off, and difficulty after difficulty thins away in front of us," said Holmes as we stood waiting for the arrival of the express train from town. "I shall soon be able to sum up one of the most unusual and sensational crimes of modern times. Students of crime-solving will remember similar incidents in Godno, in Little Russia, in the year '66, and of course there are the Anderson murders in North Carolina, but this case possesses some features which are entirely its own. Even now we have no clear case against this very clever man. But I shall be very much surprised if it is not clear enough before we go to bed tonight."

The London express came roaring into the station, and a small, wiry bulldog of a man had sprung from a first-class compartment. We all three shook hands, and I saw at once from the extremely respectful way in which Lestrade gazed at my companion that he had learned a good deal since the days when they had first worked together. I could well remember how scornfully Lestrade once viewed the reasoning abilities of Holmes.

"Anything good?" he asked.

"The biggest thing in years," said Holmes. "We have two hours before we need to think of starting. I think we might use our free time to get some dinner. Then, Lestrade, we will take the London fog out of your throat by giving you a breath of the pure night air of Dartmoor. Never been there? Ah, well, I don't suppose you will forget your first visit."

CHAPTER 14

The Hound of the Baskervilles

One of Sherlock Holmes's defects—if one may call it a defect—was that he did not like to let others know his plans until the instant they were completed. Partly it came, no doubt, from his own masterful nature. He loved to dominate and surprise those who were around him. It was also due to his professional caution, which told him never to take any chances. The result, however, was frustrating for those who were acting as his agents and assistants. I had often suffered under it, but never more so than during that long drive in the darkness. The great trial was in front of us; at last we were about to make our final effort, and yet Holmes had said nothing. I could only guess what he planned to do. My nerves thrilled with expectation when at last the cold wind on our faces and the dark, empty spaces on either side of the narrow road told me that we were back on the moor once again. Every stride of the horses and every turn of the wheels were taking us nearer to our supreme adventure.

Our conversation was hampered by the presence of the driver of the hired wagon, so that we were forced to talk of unimportant matters when our nerves were tense with emotion and anticipation. It was a relief to me, after that unnatural limitation, when we at last passed Frankland's house and knew that we were drawing near to the Hall and to the scene of action. We did not drive up to the door, but got down near the gate of the avenue. The wagon driver was paid off and ordered to return to Coombe Tracey immediately, while we started to walk to Merripit House.

"Are you armed, Lestrade?"

The little detective smiled.

"As long as I have my trousers I have a hip pocket, and as long as I have my hip pocket I have something in it."

"Good! My friend and I are also ready for emergencies."

"You're mighty tight-lipped about this affair, Mr. Holmes. What's the game now?"

"A waiting game."

"My word, it does not seem like a very cheerful place," said the detective with a shiver, glancing around him at the gloomy slopes of the hill and at the huge lake of fog which lay over the Grimpen Mire. "I see the lights of a house ahead of us."

"That is Merripit House and the end of our journey. I must request you to walk on tiptoe and not to talk above a whisper."

We moved cautiously along the path as if we were bound for the house, but Holmes halted us when we were about two hundred yards from it.

"This will do," said he. "These rocks upon the right make a fine screen."

"We are to wait here?"

"Yes, we shall make our little ambush here. Get into this hollow, Lestrade. You have been inside the house, have you not, Watson? Can you tell the position of the rooms? What are those windows at this end?"

"I think they are the kitchen windows."

"And the one beyond, which shines so brightly?"

"That is certainly the dining room."

"The blinds are up. You know the layout of the place best. Creep forward quietly and see what they are doing—but for heaven's sake don't let them know that they are being watched!"

I tiptoed down the path and stooped behind the low wall which surrounded the stunted orchard. Creeping in its shadow I reached a point whence I could look straight through the uncurtained window.

There were only two men in the room, Sir Henry and Stapleton. They sat with their profiles toward me on either side of the round table.

Both of them were smoking cigars, and coffee and wine were in front of them. Stapleton was talking in a lively way, but the baronet looked pale and upset. Perhaps the thought of that lonely walk across the ill-omened moor was weighing heavily upon his mind.

As I watched them, Stapleton rose and left the room, while Sir Henry filled his glass again and leaned back in his chair, puffing at his cigar. I heard the creak of a door and the crisp sound of boots upon gravel. The steps passed along the path on the other side of the wall under which I crouched. Looking over, I saw the naturalist pause at the door of a shed in the corner of the orchard. A key turned in a lock, and as he passed in there was a curious scuffling noise from within. He was only inside for a minute or so, and then I heard the key turn once more and he passed me and re-entered the house. I saw him rejoin his guest, and I crept quietly back to where my companions were waiting to tell them what I had seen.

"You say, Watson, that the lady is not there?" Holmes asked when I had finished my report.

"No."

"Where can she be, then, since there is no light in any other room except the kitchen?"

"I cannot think where she is."

I have said that over the great Grimpen Mire there hung a dense, white fog. It was drifting slowly in our direction and banked itself up like a wall on that side of us, low but thick and well-defined. The moon shone on it, and it looked like a great shimmering ice field, with the heads of the distant tors like rocks carried upon its surface. Holmes's face was turned toward it, and he muttered impatiently as he watched its sluggish drift.

"It's moving toward us, Watson."

"Is that serious?"

"Very serious, indeed—the one thing upon earth which could have disrupted my plans. He can't be very long, now. It is already ten o'clock. Our success and even his life may depend upon his coming out before the fog is over the path."

The night was clear and fine above us. The stars shone cold and bright, while a half-moon bathed the whole scene in a soft, uncertain light. Before us lay the dark bulk of the house, its notched roof and bristling chimneys hard outlined against the silver-spangled sky. Broad bars of golden light from the lower windows stretched across the orchard and the moor. One of them was suddenly shut off. The servants had left the kitchen. There only remained the lamp in the dining room where the two men, the murderous host and the unknowing guest, still chatted over their cigars.

Every minute that white woolly plain which covered one-half of the moor was drifting closer and closer to the house. Already the first thin wisps of it were curling across the golden square of the lighted window. The farther wall of the orchard was already invisible, and the trees were standing out of a swirl of white smoke. As we watched it, the fog-wreaths came crawling around both corners of the house and rolled slowly into one dense bank on which the upper floor and the roof floated like a strange ship upon a shadowy sea. Holmes struck his hand angrily upon the rock in front of us and stamped his feet in his impatience.

"If he isn't out in a quarter of an hour the path will be covered. In half an hour we won't be able to see our hands in front of us."

"Shall we move farther back upon higher ground?"

"Yes, I think it would be wise."

So as the fog-bank flowed onward, we fell back before it until we were half a mile from the house, and still that dense white sea, with the moon silvering its upper edge, swept slowly and unstoppably on.

"We are going too far," said Holmes. "We dare not take the chance of his being overtaken before he can reach us. At all costs we must hold our ground where we are." He dropped on his knees and clapped his ear to the ground. "Thank God, I think that I hear him coming."

A sound of quick steps broke the silence of the moor. Crouching among the stones, we stared intently at the silver-tipped bank in front of us. The steps grew louder, and through the fog, as through a curtain, there stepped the man we were waiting for. He looked around him in surprise as he emerged into the clear, starlit night. Then he came swiftly along the path, passed close to where we lay, and went on up the long slope behind us. As he walked he glanced continually over either shoulder, like a man who is extremely nervous.

"Watch!" cried Holmes, and I heard the sharp click of a cocking pistol. "Look out! It's coming!"

There was a thin, crisp, continuous patter from somewhere in the heart of that crawling fog-bank. The cloud was within fifty yards of where we lay, and we glared at it, uncertain what horror was about to break from the heart of it. I was at Holmes's elbow, and I glanced for an instant at his face. It was pale and triumphant, his eyes shining brightly in the moonlight. But suddenly they started forward in a rigid, fixed stare, and his lips parted in amazement. At the same instant Lestrade gave a yell of terror and threw himself face downward upon the ground. I sprang to my feet, my hand grasping my pistol, my mind paralyzed by the dreadful shape which had sprung out upon us from the shadows of the fog. A hound it was, an enormous coal-black hound, but not such a hound as mortal eyes have ever seen. Fire burst from its open mouth, its eyes glowed with a smoldering glare, its muzzle and neck were outlined in flickering flame. Never in the wildest dream of a madman could anything more savage, more terrible, more hellish be imagined than that dark form and savage face which broke upon us out of the wall of fog.

With long strides the huge black creature was leaping down the track, following fast upon the footsteps of our friend. So paralyzed were we by the phantom that we allowed him to pass before we had recovered our nerve. Then Holmes and I both fired together, and the creature gave a hideous howl, which showed that one at least had hit him. He did not pause, however, but bounded onward. Far away on the path we saw Sir Henry looking back, his face white in the moonlight, his hands raised in horror, glaring helplessly at the frightful thing which was hunting him down.

But that cry of pain from the hound had blown all our fears to the winds. If he could be hurt he was mortal, and if we could wound him we could kill him. Never have I seen a man run as fast as Holmes ran that night. I am considered fleet of foot, but he outran me as much as I outran Lestrade. In front of us as we flew up the track we heard scream after scream from Sir Henry and the deep roar of the hound. I was in time to see the beast spring upon its victim, hurl him to the ground and go for his throat. But the next instant Holmes had emptied five barrels of his revolver into the creature's side. With a last howl of agony and a vicious snap in the air, it rolled upon its back, four feet pawing furiously, and then fell limp upon its side. I stooped, panting, and pressed my pistol to the dreadful, shimmering head, but it was useless to press the trigger. The giant hound was dead.

Sir Henry lay unmoving where he had fallen. We tore away his collar, and Holmes breathed a prayer of gratitude when we saw that there was no sign of a wound and that the rescue had been in time. Already our friend's eyelids shivered and he made a feeble effort to move. Lestrade thrust his brandy flask between the baronet's teeth, and two frightened eyes were looking up at us.

"My God!" he whispered. "What was it? What, in heaven's name, was it?"

"It's dead, whatever it is," said Holmes. "We've laid to rest the family ghost once and for all."

In sheer size and strength it was a terrible creature which was lying stretched before us. It was not a pure bloodhound and it was not a pure mastiff; but it appeared to be a combination of the two—thin, savage, and as large as a small lioness. Even now in the stillness of death, the huge jaws seemed to be dripping with a bluish flame and the small, deep-set, cruel eyes were ringed with fire. I placed my hand upon the glowing muzzle, and as I held them up my own fingers smoldered and gleamed in the darkness.

"Phosphorus," I said.

"A clever mixture of it," said Holmes, sniffing at the dead animal. "There is no smell which might have interfered with his power of scent. We owe you a deep apology, Sir Henry, for having exposed you to this fright. I was prepared for a hound, but not for such a creature as this. And the fog gave us little time to meet him."

"You have saved my life."

"Having first endangered it. Are you strong enough to stand?"

"Give me another mouthful of that brandy and I shall be ready for anything. So! Now, if you will help me up. What do you propose to do?"

"To leave you here. You are not fit for further adventures tonight. If you will wait, one or other of us will go back with you to the Hall."

He tried to stagger to his feet; but he was still ghastly pale and trembling in every limb. We helped him to a rock, where he sat shivering with his face buried in his hands.

"We must leave you now," said Holmes. "The rest of our work must be done, and every moment is of importance. We have built our case, and now we only need to get our man."

"It's a thousand to one against our finding him at the house," he continued as we retraced our steps swiftly down the path. "Those shots must have told him that the game was up."

"We were some distance off, and this fog may have deadened them."

"He followed the hound to call him off—of that you may be certain. No, no, he's gone by this time! But we'll search the house and make sure."

The front door was open, so we rushed in and hurried from room to room to the amazement of a feeble old manservant, who met us in the passage. There was no light except in the dining room, but Holmes carried the lamp and left no corner of the house unexplored. We could see no sign of the man we were chasing. On the upper floor, however, one of the bedroom doors was locked.

"There's someone in here," cried Lestrade. "I can hear a movement. Open this door!"

A faint moaning and rustling came from within. Holmes struck the door just over the lock with the sole of his foot and it flew open. Pistol in hand, all three of us rushed into the room.

But there was no sign within of that desperate and defiant villain we expected to see. Instead we were faced by an object so strange and so unexpected that we stood for a moment staring at it in amazement.

The room had been turned into a small museum. The walls were lined by a number of glass display cases which contained a collection of butterflies and moths—the hobby of this complex and dangerous man. In the center of this room there was an upright beam, which supported the old worm-eaten beam of timber which spanned the roof. A figure was tied to this post, but it was so wrapped and muffled in the sheets that we could not tell whether it was a man or a woman. One towel passed around the throat and was knotted at the back of the pillar. Another covered the lower part of the face, and over it two dark eyes—eyes full of grief and shame and a dreadful questioning—stared back at us. In a minute we had torn off the gag, untied the bonds, and Mrs. Stapleton sank upon the floor in front of us. As her beautiful head fell upon her chest I saw the clear red welt of a whiplash across her neck.

"The brute!" cried Holmes. "Here, Lestrade, your brandy bottle! Put her in the chair! She has fainted from abuse and exhaustion."

She opened her eyes again. "Is he safe?" she asked. "Has he escaped?"

"He cannot escape us, madam."

"No, no, I did not mean my husband. Sir Henry? Is he safe?"

"Yes."

"And the hound?"

"It is dead."

She gave a long sigh of satisfaction.

"Thank God! Thank God! Oh, this villain! See how he has treated me!" She shot her arms out from her sleeves, and we saw with horror that they were all spotted with bruises. "But this is nothing—nothing! It is my mind and soul that he has tortured and defiled. I could endure it all, abuse, loneliness, a life of deception, everything, as long as I could still cling to the hope that I had his love, but now I know that in this also I have been his dupe and his tool." She broke into passionate sobbing as she spoke.

"You bear him no good will, madam," said Holmes. "Tell us then where we shall find him. If you have ever aided him in evil, help us now and so make up for it."

"There is only one place where he can have fled," she answered. "There is an old tin mine on an island in the heart of the mire. It was there that he kept his hound and there also he had made preparations so that he might have a hiding place. That is where he would run."

The fog-bank lay like white wool against the window. Holmes held the lamp towards it.

"See," said he. "No one could find his way into the Grimpen Mire tonight."

She laughed and clapped her hands. Her eyes and teeth gleamed with fierce merriment.

"He may find his way in, but never out," she cried. "How can he see the guiding wands tonight? We planted them together, he and I, to mark the pathway through the mire. Oh, if I could only have plucked them out today. Then indeed you would have had him at your mercy!"

It was clear to us that we would be unable to track him until the fog had lifted. Meanwhile we left Lestrade at the house while Holmes and I went back with the baronet to Baskerville Hall. The story about the Stapletons could no longer be withheld from him, but he took the blow bravely when he learned the truth about the woman whom he had loved. But the shock of the night's adventures had shattered his nerves, and before morning he lay delirious in a high fever under the care of Dr. Mortimer. The two of them were destined to travel together around the world before Sir Henry had become once more the strong, hearty man that he had been before he became master of that ill-omened estate.

And now I come rapidly to the conclusion of this unusual story. In telling it, I have tried to make the reader share those dark fears and vague guesses which clouded our lives so long and ended in so tragic a manner. On the morning after the death of the hound, the fog had lifted and Mrs. Stapleton guided us to the point where they had found a pathway through the bog. It helped us to realize the horror of this woman's life when we saw how eagerly and joyfully she led us on her husband's track. We left her standing upon the thin section of firm, peaty soil which tapered out into the widespread bog. From the end of it, a small wand planted here and there showed where the path zigzagged from tuft to tuft of rushes among those scummy green pits and foul swampy areas which barred the way to the stranger. Smelly reeds and lush, slimy water plants sent an odor of decay and a heavy unhealthy vapor onto our faces, while a false step plunged us more than once thigh-deep into the dark, quivering mire, which shook for yards in soft swelling around our feet. Its sticky grip plucked at our heels as we walked, and when we sank into it, it was as if some deadly hand was tugging us down into those filthy depths, so grim and purposeful was the grip in which it held us. Once only we saw a trace that someone had passed that dangerous way before us. From amid a tuft of cotton grass which bore it up out of the slime, some dark thing was sticking out. Holmes sank in up to his waist as he stepped from the path to grasp it, and if we hadn't been there to drag him out he could never have set his foot upon firm land again. He held an old black boot in the air. "Meyers, Toronto," was printed on the leather inside.

"It is worth a mud bath," said he. "It is our friend Sir Henry's missing boot."

"Thrown there by Stapleton in his flight."

"Exactly. He kept it in his hand after using it to set the hound upon the track. He fled when he knew the game was up, still clutching it. And he threw it away at this point of his flight. We know at least that he came so far in safety."

But more than that we were never destined to know, though there was much which we might guess. There was no chance of finding footsteps in the mire, for the rising mud oozed swiftly in upon them. However, as we at last reached firmer ground beyond the swamp, we all looked eagerly for them. But no slightest sign of them ever met our eyes. If the earth told a true story, then Stapleton never reached that island of safety that he struggled to get to through the fog that last night. Somewhere in the heart of the great Grimpen Mire, down in the foul slime of the huge swamp which had sucked him in, this cold and cruel-hearted man is forever buried.

We found many traces of him in the swamp-bordered island where he had hid his savage helper. A huge driving wheel and a shaft half-filled with rubbish showed the position of an abandoned mine. Beside it were the crumbling remains of the cottages of the miners, who were probably driven away by the foul smell of the surrounding swamp. In one of these a stake and chain with a pile of gnawed bones showed where the animal had been tied up. A skeleton with a tangle of brown hair sticking to it lay among the debris.

"A dog!" said Holmes. "By Jove, a curly-haired spaniel. Poor Mortimer will never see his pet again. Well, I don't believe that this place reveals any secret which we have not already guessed. He could hide his hound, but he could not quiet its voice, and from here came those cries which even in daylight were not pleasant to hear. In an emergency he could keep the hound in the shed at Merripit, but it was always a risk, and it was only on the day, the most important day, which he regarded as the end of all his efforts, that he dared do it. This paste in the can is probably the glowing mixture that he used to paint the creature. It was suggested, of course, by the story of the family hell-hound, and by the desire to frighten old Sir Charles to death. No wonder the poor devil of a convict ran and screamed, even as our friend did, and as we ourselves might have done, when he saw such a creature bounding through the darkness of the moor upon his track. It was a clever trick, for, apart from the chance of driving your victim to his death, what local person would risk asking about such a creature should he get sight of it, as many have done, out on the moor? I said it in London, Watson, and I say it again now, that never yet have we helped to hunt down a more dangerous man than he who is lying out there." As he said this, he swept his long arm toward the huge area of green-splotched bog which stretched away until it merged into the reddish-brown slopes of the moor.

CHAPTER 15

A Backward Look

It was the end of November, and Holmes and I sat, on a raw and foggy night, on either side of a blazing fire in our sitting room in Baker Street. Since the tragic upshot of our visit to Devonshire he had been engaged in two extremely important cases. In the first, he had exposed the awful conduct of Colonel Upwood in connection with the famous card scandal of the Nonpareil Club. In the second he had defended the unfortunate Mrs. Montpensier from the charge of murder which hung over her in connection with the death of her stepdaughter, Miss Carere. This young lady was found six months later alive and married in New York. My friend was in excellent spirits over the successful completion of these difficult and important cases, so that I was able to encourage him to discuss the details of the Baskerville mystery. I had waited patiently for the opportunity, since I was aware that he refused to think about old cases while working on new ones. Sir Henry and Dr. Mortimer were, however, in London, on their way to that long voyage which had been recommended to help restore his shattered nerves. They had called upon us that very afternoon, so that it was natural that the subject would come up for discussion.

"The whole course of events," said Holmes, "was, from Stapleton's point-of-view, simple and direct. To us, of course, who could only guess at his motives and actions, it all appeared tremendously complex. I have had the advantage of two conversations with Mrs. Stapleton, and the case has now been so entirely cleared up that I am not aware that there is anything which has remained a secret to us. You will find a few notes about the matter under the heading B in my indexed list of cases."

"Perhaps you would kindly give me a sketch of the course of events from memory."

"Certainly, though I cannot guarantee that I can remember all the facts. Intense mental concentration has a curious way of blotting out what has passed. So each of my cases drives out the facts of the one before it, and Miss Carere has blurred my recollection of Baskerville Hall. Tomorrow some other little problem may demand my attention. This new case, in turn, will drive out the lovely French lady and the infamous Upwood. So far as the case of the hound goes, however, I will tell you the chain of events as nearly as I can. You, then, will suggest anything which I may have forgotten."

"My investigation showed beyond all question that the family portrait did not lie, and that this fellow was indeed a Baskerville. He was a son of Rodger Baskerville, the younger brother of Sir Charles, who fled with a criminal reputation to South America, where he was said to have died unmarried. He did, as a matter of fact, marry, and had one child, this fellow, whose real name is the same as his father's. He married Beryl Garcia, one of the beauties of Costa Rica.

After stealing a large sum of public money, he changed his name to Vandeleur and fled to England, where he established a school in the east of Yorkshire. His reason for attempting this new line of work was that he had struck up an acquaintance with a sickly tutor during the voyage home. He then used this man's ability to make the new school a success. Fraser, the tutor, died however, and the school which had begun well sank from disfavor into disgrace. The Vandeleurs found it convenient to change their name to Stapleton, and he brought the remains of his fortune, his schemes for the future, and his taste for the study of insects to the south of England. I learned at the British Museum that he was recognized as an expert on the subject, and that the name of Vandeleur has been permanently attached to a certain moth which he had been the first to describe.

"We now come to that portion of his life which has proved to be of such intense interest to us. The fellow had evidently done some research and found that only two lives stood between him and ownership of a valuable estate. When he went to Devonshire his plans were, I believe, exceedingly hazy. We may infer, however, that he meant mischief from the start because of the fact that he took his wife with him and pretended that she was his sister. The idea of using her as a decoy was clearly already in his mind, though he may not have been certain how the details of his plot were to be arranged. He meant in the end to inherit the estate, and he was ready to use any tool or run any risk to reach that goal. His first act was to find a dwelling as near to his ancestral home as he could, and his second was to develop a friendship with Sir Charles Baskerville and with the neighbors.

"The baronet himself told him about the family hound, and so prepared the way for his own death. Stapleton, as I will continue to call him, knew that the old man's heart was weak and that a shock would kill him. He had learned this from Dr. Mortimer. He had heard also that Sir Charles was superstitious and had taken this grim legend very seriously. His inventive mind instantly suggested a way by which the baronet could be done to death in such a way that it would be nearly impossible to find the true murderer responsible for the crime.

"Having thought of the idea, he started to carry it out with considerable artfulness. An ordinary schemer would have been content to work with a savage hound. The use of artificial means to make the creature appear hellish was a flash of genius upon his part. The dog he bought in London from Ross and Mangles, the dealers in Fulham Road. It was the strongest and most vicious that they had. He brought it out by the North Devon line and walked a great distance over the moor so as to get it home without causing any notice. He had already learned to safely walk through the Grimpen Mire during his insect hunts, and so had found a safe hiding place for the creature. Here he kept it and waited his chance.

"But it was a long time coming. The old gentleman could not be lured outside of his grounds at night. Several times Stapleton lurked about with his hound, but with no success. It was during these fruitless quests that he, or rather his dog, was seen by some country folk, and that the legend of the demon dog received new support. He had hoped that his wife might lure Sir Charles to his ruin, but here she proved unexpectedly independent. She would not attempt to get the old gentleman involved in a romantic attachment which might deliver him over to his enemy. Threats and even, I am sorry to say, blows refused to move her. She would have nothing to do with it, and for a while Stapleton was at a deadlock.

"He eventually found a way out of his difficulties. It was a lucky break for him when Sir Charles, who had become his friend, made him the minister of his charity in the case of this unfortunate woman, Mrs. Laura Lyons. By claiming to be single, he gained power over her, and he led her to understand that if she got a divorce from her husband he would marry her. His plans were suddenly brought to a head when he learned that Sir Charles was about to leave the Hall on the advice of Dr. Mortimer, with whose opinion he himself pretended to agree. He must act at once, or his victim might get beyond his power. He therefore put pressure upon Mrs. Lyons to write this letter, begging the old man to give her an interview on the evening before his departure for London. He then, by a seemingly reasonable argument, prevented her from going, and so had the chance for which he had waited.

"Driving back in the evening from Coombe Tracey, he was in time to get his hound, to treat it with his hellish paint, and to bring the beast around to the gate at which he expected to find the old gentleman waiting. The dog, encouraged by its master, sprang over the wicket-gate and pursued the unfortunate baronet, who fled screaming down the yew alley. In that gloomy tunnel it must indeed have been a dreadful sight to see that huge black creature, with its flaming jaws and blazing eyes, bounding after its victim. He fell dead at the end of the alley from heart disease and terror. The hound had stayed upon the grassy border while the baronet had run down the path, so that no track but the man's was visible. On seeing him lying still the creature had probably approached to sniff at him, but finding him dead had turned away again. It was then that it left the print which was actually observed by Dr. Mortimer. The hound was called off and hurried away to its hiding place in the Grimpen Mire, and a mystery was left which puzzled the authorities, alarmed the countryside, and finally brought the case to our attention.

"So much for the death of Sir Charles Baskerville. You can see the devilish brilliance of it, for really it would be almost impossible to make a case against the real murderer. His only accomplice was one who could never give him away, and the horrifying, unbelievable nature of the means only served to make it more effective. Both of the women concerned in the case, Mrs. Stapleton and Mrs. Laura Lyons, were highly suspicious of Stapleton. Mrs. Stapleton knew that he had bad intentions toward the old man, and was also aware of the existence of the hound. Mrs.

Lyons knew neither of these things, but had been suspicious that the death occurred at the time of an uncancelled appointment which was only known to him. However, both women were under his control, and he had nothing to fear from them. The first half of his task was successfully completed but the more difficult still remained.

"It is possible that Stapleton did not know of the existence of an heir in Canada. In any case he would very soon learn it from his friend Dr. Mortimer, who told him details about the arrival of Henry Baskerville. Stapleton's first idea was that this young stranger from Canada might possibly be murdered in London without coming out to Devonshire at all. He distrusted his wife ever since she had refused to help him in laying a trap for the old man, and he dared not leave her out of his sight for long for fear he would lose his influence over her. It was for this reason that he took her to London with him. They stayed, I find, at the Mexborough Private Hotel, in Craven Street, which was actually one of those called upon by my helper in search of evidence. Here he kept his wife imprisoned in her room while he, disguised in a beard, followed Dr. Mortimer to Baker Street and afterward to the station and to the Northumberland Hotel. His wife had some idea of his plans; but she had such a fear of her husband—a fear founded upon brutal ill-treatment—that she dare not write to warn the man whom she knew to be in danger. If the letter should fall into Stapleton's hands, her own life would not be safe. Eventually, as we know, she adopted the means of cutting out the words which would form the message, and addressing the letter in a disguised hand. It reached the baronet, and gave him the first warning of his danger.

"It was very important for Stapleton to get some piece of Sir Henry's clothing so that, in case he was forced to use the dog, he might always have the means of setting him upon his track. With characteristic promptness and boldness he started this at once, and we cannot doubt that the hotel maid was well bribed to help him in his purpose. By chance, however, the first boot which was obtained for him was a new one and, therefore, useless for his purpose. He then had it returned and obtained another—a most instructive incident, since it proved without doubt to my mind that we were dealing with a real hound, as no other theory could explain this need to obtain an old boot and this indifference to a new one. The more peculiar an event is the more carefully it deserves to be examined. Often the very point which appears to complicate a case is, when carefully considered and scientifically handled, the one which is most likely to explain it.

"Then we received the visit from our friends

next morning, shadowed always by Stapleton in the cab. From his knowledge of our rooms and of my appearance, as well as from his general conduct, I am inclined to think that Stapleton's career of crime has been by no means limited to this single Baskerville affair. It is interesting to note that during the last three years there have been four major burglaries in the West country, yet no one was ever arrested. The last of these, at Folkestone Court, in May, was remarkable for the cold-blooded shooting of the attendant, who surprised a masked burglar. I cannot doubt that Stapleton added to his decreasing supply of money in this way, and that for years he has been a desperate and dangerous man.

"We know that he had cash on hand that morning when he got away from us so successfully. We also had an example of his lack of respect in sending back my own name to me through the cabman. From that moment he understood that I had taken over the case in London, and that therefore there was no chance for him there. He returned to Dartmoor and waited for the baronet to arrive."

"One moment!" said I. "You have, no doubt, described the sequence of events correctly, but there is one point which you have left unexplained. What became of the hound when its master was in London?"

"I have given some attention to this matter

and it is undoubtedly of importance. There can be no question that Stapleton had a helper, though it is unlikely that he ever placed himself in his power by sharing all his plans with him. There was an old manservant at Merripit House, whose name was Anthony. His connection with the Stapletons can be traced for several years, as far back as the school mastering days, so that he must have been aware that his master and mistress were really husband and wife. This man has disappeared and has escaped from the country. It is interesting to note that Anthony is not a common name in England, while Antonio is so in all Spanish or Spanish-American countries. The man, like Mrs. Stapleton herself, spoke good English, but with a curious lisping accent. I have myself seen this old man cross the Grimpen Mire by the path which Stapleton had marked out. It is very likely, therefore, that when his master was away, he cared for the hound, though he may never have known the purpose for which the beast was used.

"The Stapletons then went out to Devonshire, where they were soon followed by Sir Henry and you. One word now as to where I stood at that time. You may possibly remember that when I examined the paper upon which the printed words were fastened I looked closely for the watermark. In doing so I held it within a few inches of my eyes, and got a faint whiff of the scent known as white jessamine. There are seventy-five perfumes, and it is very important that a criminal expert should be able to tell one from the other. More than once I have worked on cases which demanded the prompt recognition of different perfumes. The scent on the paper suggested that a lady was involved. Already my thoughts began to turn toward the Stapletons. Thus I had made certain of the hound, and had guessed at the criminal before we went out to the West country.

"It was my game to watch Stapleton. It was evident, however, that I could not do this if I were with you, since he would be very much on his guard. I deceived everybody, therefore, you included, and I came out secretly when I was supposed to be in London. My hardships were not as great as you imagined, though such minor details must never interfere with the investigation of a case. I stayed for the most part at Coombe Tracey, and only used the hut on the moor when it was necessary to be near the scene of action. Cartwright had come out with me, and in his disguise as a country boy he was of great help to me. I was dependent upon him for food and clean linen. When I was watching Stapleton, Cartwright was often watching you, so that I was able to keep my hand upon all the strings.

"I have already told you that your reports reached me rapidly, since they were forwarded instantly from Baker Street to Coombe Tracey. They were a great help to me, and especially that one point when Stapleton mentioned that he had been a schoolmaster. I was able to establish the identity of the man and the woman and knew at last exactly how I stood. The case had been made more complicated through the incident of the escaped convict and his relationship to the Barrymores. This also you cleared up in a very effective way, though I had already come to the same conclusions from my own observations.

"By the time that you discovered me out on the moor I had a complete knowledge of the whole business, but I didn't have a case which could go to a jury. Even Stapleton's attempt upon Sir Henry that night which ended in the death of the unfortunate convict did not help us much in proving murder against our man. There seemed to be no choice but to catch him red-handed. To do that we had to use Sir Henry, alone and apparently unprotected, as bait. We did so, and at the cost of a severe shock to our client we succeeded in completing our case and driving Stapleton to his destruction. That Sir Henry should have been exposed to this is, I must confess, a mark against my management of the case. On the other hand, we had no means of foreseeing the terrible and paralyzing spectacle which the beast presented, nor could we predict the fog which enabled him to burst upon us at such short notice. We succeeded in our objective at a cost which both the specialist and Dr. Mortimer assure me will be a temporary one. A long journey may enable our friend to recover not only from his shattered nerves but also from his wounded feelings. His love for the lady was deep and sincere, and to him the saddest part of all this black business was that he should have been deceived by her.

"It only remains to tell of the part which she had played throughout. There can be no doubt that Stapleton had a powerful influence over her which may have been love or may have been fear, or very possibly both, since they are by no means conflicting emotions. It was, at least, totally effective. At his command she consented to pass as his sister, though he found the limits of his power over her when he attempted to make her the direct accessory to murder. She was ready to warn Sir Henry so far as she could without giving away her husband, and again and again she tried to do so. Stapleton himself seems to have been capable of jealousy. When he saw the baronet paying court to the lady, even though it was part of his own plan, he still could not help interrupting with an angry outburst. This fit of anger revealed the fiery soul which he kept cleverly concealed beneath his mild disguise. By encouraging their closeness, he made it certain that Sir Henry would often come to Merripit House and that he would sooner or later get the opportunity which he desired. On the day of the crisis, however, his wife turned suddenly against him. She had learned something of the death of the convict, and she knew that the hound was being kept in the shed on the evening that Sir Henry was coming to dinner. She accused her husband of his intended crime, and a furious scene followed in which he showed her for the first time that she had a rival in his love. Her loyalty turned in an instant to bitter hatred, and he saw that she would betray him. He tied her up so that she might have no chance of warning Sir Henry. He hoped, no doubt, that when the whole countryside blamed the baronet's death on his family's curse, as they certainly would do, he could win his wife back to accept an accomplished fact and to keep silent about what she knew. In this I believe that he made a mistake, and that, if we had not been there, his doom would nevertheless have been sealed. A woman of Spanish blood does not accept such an injury so lightly. And now, my dear Watson, without referring to my notes, I cannot give you a more detailed account of this curious case. I do not know that anything important has been left unexplained."

"He could not expect to frighten Sir Henry to death as he had done the old uncle with his phantom hound."

"The beast was savage and half-starved. If its

appearance did not frighten its victim to death, at least it would prevent him from putting up a strong fight."

"No doubt. There only remains one difficulty. If Stapleton came to inherit the fortune, how could he explain the fact that he, the heir, had been living unannounced under another name so close to the property? How could he claim it without causing suspicion and an investigation?"

"It is a very challenging difficulty, and I fear that you ask too much when you expect me to solve it. The past and the present are within the field of my investigations, but what a man may do in the future is a hard question to answer. Mrs. Stapleton has heard her husband discuss the problem on several occasions. There were three possible courses. He might claim the property from South America, establish his identity before the British authorities there and so obtain the fortune without ever coming to England at all. A second possibility was that he might adopt an elaborate disguise during the short time that he need be in London. A third possibility was that he might furnish an accomplice with the proofs and papers, putting him in as heir, and retaining a claim upon some part of his income. Based on what we know of him, it is certain that he would have found some way out of the difficulty. And now, my dear Watson, we have had many weeks of difficult work, and for one evening, I think, we may turn our thoughts to more pleasant things. I have tickets for 'The Huguenots.' Might I trouble you then to be ready in half an hour, and we can stop at Marcini's for a little dinner on the way?"

Afterword

About the Book

The Hound of the Baskervilles is an exciting mystery story which presents detective Sherlock Holmes at the height of his powers. But it is also a story which raises some thought-provoking questions. One question it asks us to think about is whether belief in the supernatural has any place in the modern world. Another question it raises is whether people can be held responsible for the crimes of their ancestors. A third question it raises is whether humanity ever progresses. Let's look at the story to see what it suggests about answers to these questions.

The plot revolves around the impact a centuries-old curse has had on a wealthy and distinguished English family, the Baskervilles. According to legend, the cruel and lustful Hugo Baskerville kidnapped a neighbor's daughter and, when she escaped, hunted her down with a pack of dogs. The young woman died of exhaustion on the moor, while Hugo, in hot pursuit, had his throat torn out by a supernatural hound from Hell. Since this violent beginning, the legend relates that all Baskerville men must be on their guard since this same vengeful "hell-hound" may appear on the lonely moor to attack them.

Recently, kindly old Sir Charles Baskerville has died under mysterious circumstances at Baskerville Hall. There were no marks on the body, but nearby were the footprints of a gigantic hound. Now his descendant, Sir Henry Baskerville, has returned to the family estate to claim his inheritance. The common folk who live on the moor believe in the old superstition and think that Sir Henry is foolish to come back. The servant couple, the Barrymores, express shock over Sir Charles's sudden death and plan to leave the gloomy old manor house as soon as Sir Henry finds someone to take their place. Even Sir Henry's new friend and neighbor, Dr. Mortimer, is torn between his belief in science and his fear of the supernatural.

Into this puzzling situation steps Sherlock Holmes, aided by his trusty sidekick, Dr. Watson. By using his powers of logical thinking, the great detective quickly concludes that Sir Henry is not being "dogged" by a supernatural hound, but by a very human enemy who is using a flesh and blood dog to terrorize the moor and Baskerville.

He reaches this conclusion after he carefully considers the incident in London where two of Sir Henry's boots are stolen from his hotel. When one of the boots—the one which has never been worn—is returned, and an older boot is stolen, Holmes correctly realizes that the old boot was taken because it bore Baskerville's scent. And who would need something that smelled like Sir Henry? Only a clever criminal who needed the boot so that he could set a real life hound on his trail. In other words, a criminal like the seemingly harmless butterfly collector, Stapleton.

Skillful author that he is, Doyle doesn't let us in on the fact that Holmes has already concluded that a real animal is involved. Nor does Holmes immediately tell Watson of his suspicions. Instead he prolongs the suspense. We readers are treated to the moody atmosphere that Dr. Watson encounters on the moor. Key "ingredients" that the author uses to create this atmosphere are the barren moor landscape, dreary weather, an escaped murderer, prehistoric ruins, suspicious servants, swamps that devour animals whole, and of course, the mournful howl of what sounds like a ghostly hound. Is it any wonder that we, as well as Dr. Watson, half believe that there may be some truth to the horrifying superstition?

Of course, in the end logic wins out. Sherlock Holmes exposes the greedy Stapleton for what he is: a long-lost Baskerville relative with a criminal past who seeks to drive Sir Henry to his death so that he may claim the Baskerville fortune. His trickery is exposed when Holmes shoots and kills the enormous dog, whose muzzle had been painted with phosphorus so that it appeared more terrifying in the dark. His plot foiled, Stapleton meets a fitting end when he is apparently swallowed up by the treacherous slime of Grimpen Mire. Other loose threads are tied up as Watson and Holmes discuss the case back at their cozy apartment at 221B Baker Street in London.

In recounting how Sherlock Holmes solved the case, author Doyle seems to be suggesting that humanity has progressed since prehistoric times when life was a primitive struggle for survival. In order to defeat his brutal enemy and solve the case, Sherlock Holmes must be willing to spend time in a prehistoric dwelling out on the moors. By having his fictional hero do this, Doyle seems to be telling us that humanity can continue to enjoy the benefits of civilization only if we are willing to use our reasoning power and our sense of compassion to confront our negative instincts—superstitious fear and murderous greed. Although Stapleton has reasoning ability too, he uses his powers in the service of a negative emotion: greed. Holmes, on the other hand, uses his intellectual ability to come to the aid of Sir Henry Baskerville. His powers of logical deduction also work for the good as they enable Stapleton's wife to become free from the clutches of her violently abusive husband.

As the story concludes, Doyle also seems to be telling us that people should not be held accountable for the sins of their ancestors. Certainly kindly old Sir Charles Baskerville, whose goal was to use his money to help the poor moorland folk, did not deserve his tragic fate. Nor does the brave, generous, self-disciplined Henry Baskerville seem in any way deserving of punishment. That's what makes his rescue by the masterful detective Sherlock Holmes so satisfying.

About the Author

Often the creator of a literary character identifies with his creation, who may possess qualities that the author admires. But even though fictional detective Sherlock Holmes was beloved the world over for his ability to solve even the most difficult mysteries, his creator, Sir Arthur Conan Doyle, had mixed feelings about him. Let's look at Doyle's life to see why this was so.

Arthur Conan Doyle was born in Edinburgh, Scotland in 1859. Both of Doyle's parents were Roman Catholics who had emigrated from Ireland in search of economic opportunities.

Doyle's father, Charles, was a government worker who also worked part-time at illustrating books and doing sketches of criminal trials. Unfortunately for his family, he was also a heavy drinker whose behavior became so unstable that he was eventually institutionalized. However, his wealthy relatives, among them the successful illustrator Richard Doyle, saw to it that young Arthur received an education. The boy was sent to a Catholic boarding school, Stonyhurst, at the age of nine and stayed until he was sixteen. He disliked the strict routine and harsh discipline of the school, but became popular with his fellow students due to his wonderful storytelling abilities. Doyle himself credited his mother, Mary, with awakening his interest in literature because of her own ability to relate fascinating stories. She was a highly cultured woman who kept the family afloat financially by running a boarding house when her husband could no longer hold a job. Her son Arthur revered her throughout his life.

After Doyle left Stonyhurst, he studied medicine at the University of Edinburgh from 1876 to 1881. He had mixed feelings about studying medicine—on one hand he loved literature, but on the other, he felt he should study something which would ensure that he could earn a good living. Additionally, he was influenced by Dr. Bryan Charles Waller, a young lodger his mother had taken in to make ends meet. Waller had studied at the University of Edinburgh. As things worked out, his study of medicine aided him in the creation of his most famous fictional character; for it was here that he met Professor Joseph Bell, whose powerful intellectual abilities became the model for Sherlock Holmes.

Following his term at the University, Doyle served as a ship's doctor on a voyage to the West African coast. In 1882 he set up a private practice in Portsmouth, England. During this time he struggled to build up his medical practice but also worked at becoming a recognized author. It was at this time, also, that he married a young woman named Louisa Hawkins.

Doyle's first novel about Holmes, *A Study in Scarlet,* was published in 1887. The second Sherlock Holmes story, *The Sign of Four,* was written for *Lippincott Magazine.* In July, 1891, the *Strand Magazine* began to publish installments of "The Adventures of Sherlock Holmes." The stories were an overwhelming success and Holmes's address of 221B Baker Street in London became probably the most famous address in literature. Yet by now, the differences between Doyle and his fictional creation were becoming obvious. By the end of 1891, Doyle was planning to abandon the Holmes stories and kill off his fictional detective. Why? He viewed the Sherlock Holmes stories as "commercial" at best and resented the fact that they took him away from writing the historical novels he considered more important. In 1893, Doyle devised Holmes's death at the hands of his arch-enemy, Professor Moriarty, in the story entitled "The Final Problem." Twenty-thousand readers of the *Strand Magazine*, where the story appeared, responded by canceling their subscriptions. Some even wore mourning bands to demonstrate their grief at Holmes's "death." Despite the public outcry, Doyle felt liberated by the death of his fictional creation and immersed himself in other work. His high spirits were short-lived, however, as his wife Louisa was diagnosed with tuberculosis, which was then an often fatal disease. The stress of caring for her coupled with his father's death threw Doyle into a depression which may have increased his interest in the supernatural. He had long been attracted to Spiritualism, a movement whose followers believed that it was possible to communicate with the spirits of the deceased. When he joined the Society for Psychical Research, the public considered it a public declaration of his interest and belief in the occult. In the years that followed, Doyle's belief in the supernatural made him the target of much ridicule, yet it didn't undermine his beliefs. Throughout his life, he continued to give lectures on the subject and gave money to various groups so that they could further explore psychic phenomena.

In 1897, Doyle met the woman who would eventually become his second wife. Jean Leckie was young, beautiful, and far more intellectual than most women of the time. Doyle was instantly attracted to her. The feeling was mutual but the two did not wed until a year after the death of Louisa, which took place in 1906.

Around the same time he met Jean Leckie, Doyle wrote a play about Sherlock Holmes, not because he wanted to, but because he needed the money. The play was a huge success and left Doyle free to attend to his other interests, which included serving as a medical doctor during the Boer War in South Africa. When Doyle returned from that adventure, he threw himself into politics and narrowly lost when he ran for a seat in the British parliament.

The inspiration for his next novel came after a prolonged visit to the Devonshire moor. While on vacation, he learned the legend of a huge, ghostlike hound. Realizing that the story and setting would form an ideal challenge for Sherlock Holmes, Doyle wrote *The Hound of the Baskervilles* as if it was a previously untold adventure of the deceased detective. Holmes fans were delighted and the novel became a worldwide sensation when the first chapters were serialized in the *Strand Magazine* in 1901.

Doyle continued writing more Holmes stories in response to pressure put on him by his public. Yet he continued to be interested in other things, including fast cars, airplanes, and hot air balloons. He demonstrated his compassion for the underdog when he became involved in several cases where he believed men had been convicted of crimes they didn't commit. Several prisoners were released due to Doyle's involvement in their causes.

A year after Louisa died, Doyle and Jean Leckie got married in September 1907. The marriage was a happy one. In addition to his two children with Louisa, Doyle became the father of three more children with Jean—two sons and a daughter. Doyle continued his fiction writing by creating the Professor Challenger books. One, *The Lost World*, involved a group of explorers who travel to a remote region of South America and encounter dinosaurs—many years before *Jurassic Park*.

In 1914 World War I began. Doyle offered to enlist in the British army, but at age fifty-five, he was rejected. Still, the war exacted an awful toll on the author. His son, Kingsley, his brother, two brothers-in-law, and two nephews were all killed in the war. Some feel that these shattering losses contributed to Doyle's profound interest in Spiritualism. Certainly his belief that mediums could communicate with the dead must have provided some consolation for the grieving author. His wife came to share his beliefs and accompanied him on his lectures and meetings with fellow believers. After 1918, Doyle wrote very little fiction, writing about Spiritualism instead. In 1921 he wrote a book entitled *The Coming of the Fairies* which argued that fairies and spirits actually exist.

So we see that Arthur Conan Doyle was not at all like the emotionally cool, extremely rational man that his fictional detective was. Unlike Holmes, who in *The Hound of the Baskervilles*, regards the legend of the Baskerville curse as a "fairy tale," Doyle actually believed in the supernatural. In keeping with his beliefs, Doyle viewed death not as an ending but as "the greatest and most glorious adventure of all." He died peacefully on July 7, 1930, surrounded by his family.

At one point in *The Hound of the Baskervilles*, Sherlock Holmes disapprovingly says to Dr. Mortimer: "I see you have gone over to the supernaturalists." We might say the same of Holmes's creator.